BL

"Now then, White Hair," Palacio said. "To what do I owe the pleasure of your visit?"

"Desperation," Col. Reynolds said. "I want to stop the White Apache once and for all."

"We share the same dream," Palacio said, his countenance clouding. "But we have tried many times and he is still alive."

"I have a new idea," Reynolds said. "I want to make one of your people very rich."

"Rich?"

"Yes. Do you think any of them would like to own eight new horses, forty new blankets, six new knives, an ax, and all the tobacco he can carry?"

The vision of so much wealth made Palacio's head spin. "Who would not?"

"Excellent. All those things will be given to the warrior who tells me where White Apache and Delgadito are hiding."

Palacio had to bite his lip to keep from howling for sheer joy. "Never fear, White Hair. The renegades are as good as dead."

The *White Apache* series by *Leisure Books:*

6

**BLOOD
TREACHERY**

**Jake
McMasters**

LEISURE BOOKS   **NEW YORK CITY**

To Judy, Joshua, and Shane.

A LEISURE BOOK®

February 1995

Published by

Dorchester Publishing Co., Inc.
276 Fifth Avenue
New York, NY 10001

Printed in the United States of America.

Chapter One

Cpl. Jim Ralston was a dead man but he didn't know it yet.

The day had started the same as the past five. The young soldier had risen at the crack of dawn, downed several cups of scalding black coffee, chewed a few tangy pieces of beef jerky, and climbed on his mount as the blazing sun cleared the golden eastern horizon.

Once again Ralston rode steadily deeper into the Chiricahua Mountains. Common sense told him that he should turn around and hightail it back to Fort Bowie. Simple logic made it plain that a lone trooper had a snowball's chance in hell of tracking down the most feared renegade in all of Arizona Territory. But then he thought of the ten-thousand dollars being offered for the White Apache, dead or alive, and he shook his head to dispel his doubts.

Ten-thousand dollars was more than Ralston

could expect to make in a lifetime. Having that much money meant he could say adios to the stark military life he had lived for seven years. He could head back to the States and set himself up in a fine house. Maybe he'd even find himself a pretty woman who would be willing to settle down and spend the rest of her nights giving him back rubs and her days darning his socks.

Of such fancies are dreams made. And Cpl. Ralston's dream explained why he had taken the two weeks' furlough he had earned, loaded up a pack mule, and headed into the Chiricahua Apache Reservation.

The trooper knew he had disobeyed a standing order. Headquarters, Fifth Cavalry, had sent a dispatch to all commands. Under no circumstances were soldiers to enter the Reservation without the express consent of their superiors. Anyone who violated the edict stood the risk of being court-martialed.

It had taken a score of years and the loss of many lives before the U.S. government had been able to bring the fierce Chiricahuas to bay. The tribe had only agreed to live on a reservation after their revered leader Cochise wrangled a promise from Washington; the heart of Chiricahua country, the Dragoon and Chiricahua Mountains, was to belong to the Chiricahuas for all time.

Since the treaty had gone into effect, there had been scattered incidents. Many of the younger warriors resented living under the white man's yoke. A few had turned renegade and many more would if provoked, so the government bent over backwards to insure they weren't. Whiskey traders were kept off the reservation—but managed to smuggle their wares in anyway. Prospectors were barred from looking for color in the mountains—

but scores did so and were rarely caught. And soldiers were to fight shy of the Chiricahuas or suffer the consequences.

But how could anyone in his right mind pass up a crack at ten-thousand dollars? Ralston asked himself as he crested a barren ridge. He certainly couldn't, and he knew of other soldiers who felt the same way but lacked the grit to try and claim the money.

Besides, the corporal doubted the government would raise much of a ruckus if someone rode into the fort with the body of the White Apache draped over a saddle. Washington didn't care how the terror of the Southwest was brought down, just so someone made wolf meat of him before he stirred the Chiricahuas up enough to incite them to out-and-out war.

No, sir, Ralston mused. The man who brought in the savage killer would be hailed as a hero, no questions asked. His story would be in all the papers. He'd be famous in no time. So what if a few rules were bent in the doing of the deed? It was the result that counted.

The burning sun had bought beads of sweat to Corporal Ralston's forehead. He wiped the back of his sleeve across his brow, pushed his hat back on his head, and unslung his canteen to take a sip. As he raised it to his parched lips, he caught a glimmer of light on the rocky slope to the west, no more than a pinpoint flash.

Instantly replacing the canteen, Ralston moved behind a boulder the size of a log cabin. Twisting in the saddle, he opened his saddlebags and took out a small spyglass he had bought at the sutler's. He unfolded the telescope and pressed it to his right eye.

Nothing moved on the slope. Whatever had

caused the flash was either gone, or so well hidden as to be invisible.

Ralston suspected the latter. The glimmer had been caused by sunlight reflecting off metal, most likely a rifle or a knife. And odds were that the rifle or knife had an Apache attached to it.

Wedging the spyglass under his wide leather belt, the corporal drew his carbine from the boot and fed a round into the chamber. He had to remind himself not to do anything rash. It might be a tame buck out hunting, although the odds were slim given that he was so far into the wilderness and the tame bucks liked to stay closer to the reservation proper.

Deciding to play it safe, Ralston rode back over the crest of the ridge and along it to a point directly across from the spot where he had seen the flash. He drew rein, dismounted, and ground-hitched his animal. The mule he tied to a manzanita, since it had a tendency to wander off.

The corporal stuffed extra ammunition into his pockets, then climbed to the top. He eased onto his belly behind a small boulder and scanned the vicinity. To his left a lizard scuttled across the baked earth into the shade of a cactus. It was the only sign of life to be seen.

Arizona was a hard land and it bred hard men, white and red. Ralston wasn't fooling himself. He realized that he was up against one of the most dangerous men alive. And it would take dumb luck, as much as anything else, for him to put an end to the White Apache's rampage.

According to the post commander, the White Apache had once been a respectable rancher named Clay Taggart. He had gone bad, though, in a big way. First he'd tried to rape the wife of a neighbor and killed one of the hands who came to her rescue. Then, on the run from the law, he'd hooked up with Delgadito, a genuine Apache renegade who had been the most wanted savage in the Territory until Taggart came along.

It was hard for Ralston to imagine. He couldn't see any white man pairing up with any red devil. In his eyes it was a crime against human nature, a perversion of all that he believed in. Apaches were little better than animals. Everyone knew that. Which made any white who would side with them a traitor to his own kind.

The corporal shut such thoughts from his mind and concentrated on the slope. When tangling with Apaches, the rule of thumb was to shoot first and think later. He brought the telescope into play again but the result was the same as before.

Minutes dragged by. The heat was stifling. Ralston's uniform clung to him when he moved. He would have given anything to enjoy a nice, long cold bath—and he wasn't a big believer in baths. Once every three months or so was enough to keep him clean and in the flush of health. Take baths too often, his grandpa used to say, and a body would wind up sickly.

Ralston frowned, certain he was wasting his time. He figured the Apache was long gone. He would be better off forking leather and riding on. Putting his hand down, he pushed to his knees and started to turn. As he did so, he saw an Apache standing less than ten feet away with an arrow notched to a sinew bowstring.

The trooper acted on sheer instinct. Throwing himself to the right, he leveled the carbine and snapped off a shot while in midair. More by luck than design the Apache was hit squarely in the chest and staggered backward.

Even as Ralston hit the ground he clawed at his revolver. He rolled a few feet in case the stricken warrior managed to loose the arrow while thumbing back the hammer of his Colt. Suddenly stopping, he saw the warrior sinking to the ground as if mortally wounded. But Ralston was taking no chances. He fired three times. The blast echoed off the nearby mountains, resembling a cannonade.

At each retort the Apache jerked with the impact of the bullet. With the third shot, he pitched onto his face and lay as still as a log.

Ralston slowly rose, keeping the warrior covered. His blood raced, his temples pounded. It had all happened so fast that only now did his brain begin to function as it should. Walking over, he nudged the dead Apache with the tip of his boot. When there was no reaction, he bent and flipped the warrior over.

Only then did Ralston realize it was a boy, no more than fourteen or fifteen years old. The boy had no knife, no tomahawk. The bow was old. The arrow lacked a barbed tip, and it was the only shaft the boy had. Belatedly, Ralston recalled that the youngster had not held the bow ready to shoot but rather had held it low down, at his side, with the arrow angled at the ground.

Ralston slowly holstered the pistol. It occurred to him that the boy wasn't a renegade, that he had just slain a young tame buck out hunting.

Some men would have felt deep remorse. Many would have regretted what they had done. The corporal merely kicked the boy in the side and muttered, "You damn redskin. That's what you get for sneaking up on me the way you did."

Abruptly, Ralston had a troubling thought.

10

What if the youngster had been a member of a hunting party? Crouching behind a boulder with his carbine in hand, he surveyed the length and breadth of the mountainous terrain but saw no reason for alarm. When enough time went by to convince him the youngster had been alone, he rose and hurried to where he had left the horse and the mule.

Stepping into the stirrups, Ralston set off at a brisk pace northward. He had to get out of there. The sound of the shots had no doubt carried a long distance and might prompt other Apaches to investigate.

For the better part of the morning the corporal forged his solitary way into the Chiricahua homeland. He marveled for the umpteenth time at the Apache ability to endure in a harsh, arid land fit only for sidewinders, gila monsters, and scorpions. It was no wonder the Apaches were noted for being as tough as the creatures with which they shared their land.

Shortly before noon, Ralston rode over a crest into a heavily forested tract bordering a narrow, fertile valley. It was a virtual oasis. He made toward a meandering stream with a smile of anticipation on his face.

At the water's edge, the corporal climbed down, knelt, removed his hat, and plunged his entire head into the cool, invigorating water. Rising up, he laughed lightly and shook himself to clear his eyes. Then he drank, gulping even though he knew it was wiser to sip slowly after blistering in the intense heat for so long. He couldn't help himself.

Once Ralston had slaked his thirst, he walked over to a tree and sat with his back to the trunk. His horse still guzzled greedily, as he had, but the mule had moved off a few yards to graze. Mules were smarter than horses in that respect; they never drank so much that they swelled up like a waterbag fit to burst and became too waterlogged to move.

Ralston toyed with the notion of going over and dragging his mount out of the stream, but he couldn't motivate himself to make the effort. Sitting in the shade with a faint breeze chilling his damp skin felt so glorious, he had no desire to budge. Besides which, he had decided on the spur of the moment to spend the night there. Sources of water were few and far between. He intended to make the most of this one while he had the chance.

Accordingly, after briefly dozing, Ralston stripped off his cartridge belt and his uniform, then waded into the stream in his birthday suit. A convenient pool, about knee-deep, gave him the perfect spot to plop down. The water rose to just under his chin, and for the first time in more days than he could remember, he wasn't sweating from head to toe. It felt wonderful.

"Almost makes a man wish he was a fish," Ralston said aloud to himself. He moved closer to the bank to be within quick reach of the carbine and the revolver, which he had placed at the water's edge.

Both the horse and mule were cropping grass. Neither betrayed any skittishness, as they would if they had caught the scent of an Indian or a beast.

Ralston allowed himself to relax fully for the first time that day. He leaned his head back onto the bank and closed his eyes, relying on the animals to warn him if a threat loomed. Off to the northeast a bird shrieked, prompting him to crack his lids and look. A red hawk soared high on the currents, wheeling in search of prey.

They had a lot in common, Ralston thought. They were both alone. They were both hunters. They both relied on their wits to survive. He watched the big bird soar for a while, then dozed off. A dream came to him in which he grew great wings and flew into the air like an avenging human hawk. Soon the White Apache appeared below. He swooped down and grasped the renegade in razor-sharp talons. Ripping and rending, he tore the White Apache to ribbons. The renegade died screaming.

Ralston came awake slowly, savoring a feeling of lassitude. Something pricked him ever so lightly on the left shoulder. It felt like the bite of a small insect. He idly reached up and ran his hand over the spot but felt nothing.

Once more the corporal was pricked, this time on the forearm. Reluctantly, he opened his eyes and stared at his wrist. He was surprised to see a tiny drop of blood.

A sharper prick lanced the side of Ralston neck. Immediately he slapped at himself, thinking that maybe a bee or a hornet was responsible. But then his hand was seared by a strange burning pain and when he lowered his arm, he discovered that two of his fingers were gone. Blood squirted into the stream, turning the water a murky rust color.

Startled, Cpl. Ralston twisted to see what was behind him and nearly passed out from shock. He tried to jump to his feet but his legs refused to cooperate. So stunned was he that for the moment he forgot about his missing fingers.

A man stood there, holding a Bowie knife. He

was tall, well proportioned, and superbly muscled. His body had been bronzed by the sun until it was the same hue as an Apache's. His long black hair was also typical of an Apache's, as were the breechcloth and style of moccasins he wore. Slanted across his chest, Indian fashion, was a bandoleer brimming with cartridges. Slung over his left shoulder was a Winchester. On his right hip, in a Mexican holster decorated with silver studs, rode a fancy nickel-plated pistol.

Unlike Apaches, the man wore a wide-brimmed brown hat such as prospectors favored, the front brim curled up so he could see clearly. And in marked contrast to any Apache who had ever lived, the man's eyes were a striking lake-blue.

Ralston knew who it was. Recognition shattered his shock and he turned to grab his Colt, which had been inches away. But the revolver and the carbine were gone.

"Are you looking for those, soldier boy?" the apparition asked in a deep voice, and pointed at the weapons that had been placed a dozen feet off, well out of his reach. "I moved them while you slept."

The corporal couldn't conceive of anyone being so light on his feet. He glanced at the horse and mule, which grazed on as if nothing out of the ordinary had taken place.

The man noticed and smiled. "I know what you're thinking. Calvary horses usually act up when they smell Apaches. But I'm not an Apache."

"I know who you are," Ralston blurted more harshly than he would have liked. It was then that sheer agony coursed through him as he belatedly felt the full effect of having his fingers sliced off. He pressed the stubs against his side

14

and shuffled awkwardly to his feet, heedless of his nakedness. "What do you want?" he stupidly asked, well aware of the answer before he posed the question.

"Why the boy?"

"I don't know what you're—" Ralston began, and yipped like a gut-shot coyote when the Bowie leaped out and ripped a four-inch gash in his left shoulder.

"Why did you kill the boy?"

Ralston, grimacing, back-pedaled. Desperate for salvation, he looked to right and left for something he could use to defend himself.

"I heard the shots, blue-belly," the renegade had gone on casually. "I found the body and read the sign. You had no call to gun him down."

"I did!" the corporal responded, his voice strident with fear he could scarcely hide. "He was trying to kill me!"

"Liar. His name was Eskaminzin. His cousin, Ponce, rides with me and every so often Eskaminzin would pay us a visit. We tried to get him to join our band, but he always refused. He said that he didn't hate the whites as much as we do."

Ralston had gone the width of the stream. He halted, shut the torment from his mind, and willed his nerves to steady. "I tell you that he left me no choice!" he lied. "You have to believe me. I'm not one of those who go around making wolf meat of Apaches for the hell of it."

"What are you doing here, then?"

There was no earthly reason, other than hunting Apaches or prospecting, for any white man to be in that part of the reservation, and Ralston knew it. "I had some time on my hands," he said, "and I heard tell that there might be gold up in these mountains."

"So you're playing prospector, is that it?"

"Yes," Ralston said, nodding vigorously. The White Apache didn't strike him as being anywhere near as bloodthirsty as he had been led to believe. With a little luck, he was sure he could talk his way out of the fix he was in.

"That's mighty peculiar," the tall man said. "I don't see any prospecting gear on your mule, yonder. No shovel, no pick, no pan. What exactly are you prospecting with? Your picket pin?"

Ralston swallowed to moisten his dry throat. "I didn't say I aimed to do any digging this trip. I'm just looking around to see if I can find some color."

The scourge of the Territory sighed and squatted to wipe the Bowie clean on the grass. "There was a time when I would have given you the benefit of the doubt, mister. But I've learned better, the hard way. I know you're lying through your teeth. And so do they."

"They?"

"Oh. Where are my manners? I forgot to introduce my pards. Take a gander behind you."

Cpl. Ralston did, and his heart pounded madly in his chest. Four full-blooded Apaches flanked him. Four heavily armed, somber-as-death-itself, swarthy Apaches whose features were as flinty as quartz.

Until that moment, the trooper had been under the impression that one Apache looked just about the same as every other. It had been hard for him to tell them apart, even the Apache scouts who worked for the Cavalry and rode out with every patrol.

This time it was different. Perhaps due to his

predicament, which had sharpened his senses to their utmost, he saw four individuals standing before him, not four faceless savages.

The one on the right was the youngest. He wore a blue shirt and brown vest, and his eyes blazed hatred.

Next there was a slender warrior partial to a gray shirt. Above the top of the cartridge-belt strapped around his waist jutted a large black knife-hilt.

The third warrior had an air about him. His eyes were like those of an eagle, his expression that of a man who exercised supreme self-control.

Last of all was a square-shouldered bear of a warrior with fiery eyes and a nasty scar in the shape of a lightning bolt on his brow. This one sneered and stood hunched forward, resembling a grizzly about to pounce.

"That young one there is Ponce," the man across the stream said. "He's a mite riled that you killed his cousin. Next to him is Cuchillo Negro, or Black Knife as the whites like to call him. Then there's Delgadito. I reckon you've heard of him."

Overcome by unbridled terror, all Ralston could do was nod.

"As for that friendly cuss on the end, he's called Fiero. It shouldn't be hard to figure out why."

The corporal edged back into the middle of the stream. He had never felt so vulnerable in all his born days, and he swore his knees quaked as he said, "You've got to help me, Taggart. You can't stand by and let these butchers do what they want."

"It's out of my hands, soldier boy. I might be the leader of the band, but that doesn't give me the right to boss them around as I see fit. Apaches do as they please, when they please."

17

The one called Fiero moved toward the bank but stopped at a word from Delgadito, who glanced at the young warrior, Ponce. Ponce then stalked forward, a war club at his side.

"Oh, God!" Ralston cried, goose bumps breaking out all over his body. He fought down an urge to scream and retreated a few strides. "Tell them they can have my horse and mule, my supplies and guns and everything! All they have to do is let me live."

The renegade chuckled. "I think you're missing the point, pilgrim. They're going to take all your stuff anyway. After Ponce, there, bashes in your skull, of course. Then Fiero will likely skin you. He likes to make pouches out of white hides ever since he killed a trooper who had made a tobacco pouch out of the breast of an Apache woman." He paused. "After that, Delgadito and Cuchillo Negro will probably cut you into little pieces and scatter the parts around for the wild critters to eat. All I'll wind up with is the head, but that will be enough."

Cpl. Jim Ralston wanted to ask what Taggart meant by that remark, but his vocal cords were paralyzed. In fact, his entire frame had frozen of its own accord, and all he could do was stand there and tremble like a terrified mouse as the young avenger with the war club sprang high into the air and swooped down toward him just as he had swooped down on the White Apache in his dream. The last sight he saw was that of the heavy war club streaking toward his forehead. It grew larger and larger until, for a fleeting fraction of an instant, the war club seemed to fill the sky from end to end.

And then the world exploded.

Chapter Two

Fort Bowie sat on a hill in the Chiricahua Mountains on the eastern approach to Apache Pass. It had been built to insure that travelers using the Tucson-Mesilla road could do so in safety, and to safeguard a crucial spring, the only source of water for many miles around.

Careerwise, it was the bottom of the Army barrel, the post of last resort. Troopers from Maine to California dreaded being sent to Bowie, and when assigned, generally despised every miserable minute. The heat, the isolation, the hard work, they all made life a living hell. And as if that weren't enough, there was the constant threat of attack by renegades. Soldiers riding out on routine patrol never knew if they would live to see the high ramparts again.

So the troopers hated Fort Bowie. And their commanding officer was no exception. Colonel Thomas Reynolds stood outside the headquarters building and gazed with clear distaste at the dusty parade ground. In all his years of military service, he had never loathed any assignment so much as he did being sent to Bowie.

Reynolds had only himself to blame. He had blundered at his previous post and allowed a patrol to be needlessly wiped out by Sioux. Less than a month later new orders had arrived, dispatching him to Arizona Territory. Coincidence? Some would say so. Reynolds knew better. The Army frowned on incompetence. Those who didn't measure up to standard were thrown to the wolves.

But as the old saying went, there was a silver lining to every cloud. In this case, Reynolds had a chance to redeem himself if he could last his tour at Bowie without making any more boneheaded blunders—and if he could keep the Apaches in line.

So far, the colonel had not made any mistakes. But he was finding it harder by the day to keep a lid on the festering cauldron of the Chiricahua Reservation. Thanks to renegades like Delgadito and the White Apache, the potential for a mass uprising was greater than at any time since the death of Cochise.

Reynolds pulled his hat brim low against the sun and headed across the compound. He thought of all that had been done to avert war, and what needed to be done if the fragile peace was to hold.

Washington had done its typical inane bit to help. Shortly after the Chiricahua Reservation had been formed, word came down that henceforth Fort Bowie would be known as *Camp* Bowie. The political logic had been instructive. Since the post was located smack in the middle of the Chiricahua reserve, Washington had felt the tribe might resent its presence. But instead of dismantling the post and moving it outside the reservation, the higher-ups decided to simply rename it.

Who did they think they were fooling? Reynolds often mused. Washington could call it a camp if they wanted, but everyone at the post, and everyone in Arizona, still called it a fort. So, too, did the Apaches, who were a lot smarter than the politicians gave them credit for being.

Col. Reynolds came to the small building that housed the office of the Chief of Scouts. Without bothering to knock, he threw the door wide and walked in.

Caught in the act of raising a silver flask to his lips was Capt. Vincent Parmalee. Thin as a rail, with a sallow complexion from too much time spent indoors, Parmalee had made no secret of the fact he resented being picked to supervise "a bunch of filthy, ignorant heathens," as he called them. Nor was it a secret that he drowned his resentment in a bottle.

"I trust you're drinking water, Captain," Reynolds said stiffly. On several occasions he had warned Parmalee about being under the influence while on duty. Just as he had warned a score of others guilty of the same offense.

Alcoholism was rampant among the soldiers there, a consequence of the brutal conditions under which they lived. It was the only way many of them got through the day, and Reynolds knew that trying to stamp it out would be like trying to stamp out a raging forest fire. The best he could do was sweep it under the rug and only punish blatant offenders.

Parmalee stiffened as if snake bit and lowered

the flask into an open drawer. "Sir!" he exclaimed. Rising, he snapped to attention. "Of course it is, Colonel."

Frowning, Reynolds walked around the desk, picked up the flask, and held it under his nose. "Since when is spring water one hundred proof?" He held out his arm and upended the contents. "I've been lenient with you, Captain, because I sympathize with your plight. Let me catch you one more time, however, and you'll spend a few days in the guardhouse."

Captain Parmalee grit his teeth to keep from spitting out the string of curses he wanted to utter. He thought it unfair and cruel for his superior to begrudge him a few nips. But he wasn't about to risk having an official reprimand placed on his record. He already had too many. one or two more and he might be tossed out of the Army on his ear, and he only needed to tough it out for another eight years and he could retire with a small pension. Enough to keep him in whiskey the rest of his life.

"I'll get straight to the point," Reynolds said, placing the flask on the desk. "What's the latest on the renegades?"

"There's nothing new to report, sir," Parmalee said. "The scouts are doing their best but they have no idea where White Apache and Delgadito have hid out." He wasn't one to offer excuses for the savages serving under him, but at the same time he didn't care to have their poor performance reflect on his, so he added, "You have to bear in mind the size of the reservation, sir. It would take the entire Fifth Army a full year just to check every nook and cranny in the Dragoons, let alone the Chiricahua Mountains."

"Don't lecture me on the difficulties," Reynolds

replied. "I'm fully aware that the Apaches know these mountains as they do the backs of their hands. If your scouts haven't found the renegades, it's because they don't want to find them."

Parmalee opened his mouth to argue but thought better of the idea. The colonel was only saying what they both knew to be true.

"This impasse is intolerable," Reynolds continued. "If the scouts you have won't do their job, then dismiss the shirkers and sign up a new bunch."

"It's not that simple, sir," Parmalee said. "If we give the scouts the boot without a damn good reason, they're liable to hold a grudge. And once word spreads, there won't be a buck anywhere willing to work for us."

"Then what—" Colonel Reynolds began, but stopped when shouts broke out in the direction of the main gate. Boots pounded, and the piercing wail of a bugle rent the air. "Damn!" he said, speeding from the office with the captain on his heels.

The entire fort was in an uproar. Troopers were rushing toward the gate. Others were scaling ladders to the parapets. Still others were just emerging from their barracks, pulling on clothes as they ran or loading carbines on the fly.

From out of the midst of the confusion jogged a burly noncom. Sergeant Joe McKinn halted, saluted, and declared, "A sentry in guard tower two claims he saw several Apaches within spitting distance of the post, sir."

"Was that cause to call out the whole garrison?" Reynolds demanded, not a little peeved. He had lost count of the number of times the alarm had been sounded only to turn out to be false.

McKinn didn't bat an eye. "They left us a present, sir. Another one of *those.*"

"Damn. Lead the way."

The sergeant did so with exquisite precision. He plowed through the milling troopers like a man-of-war through a turbulent sea, bellowing orders as he ran, rendering drilled order out of confused chaos. At the base of a ladder he stepped aside to permit his superiors to go ahead of him, and craned his head back to see the sentry. "Private Gibbs! Any more sign of Apaches?"

"Not a trace, Sarge."

McKinn was glad. He had already lost one commanding officer in his career and he had no intention of losing another. He noted with satisfaction that most of the troopers were at their positions, weapons at the ready. Any Apache foolhardy enough to fire a shot from close up would be shot to ribbons in the blink of an eye.

The two officers gained the senty tower, which was unlike most of its kind. But for that matter, so was the entire post.

Fort Bowie had been built in an arid area almost devoid of trees. So instead of having an outer palisade constructed of high wooden poles, as did the majority of Western posts, Bowie boasted walls of stone so thick no bullet could penetrate, and against which arrows and lances shattered on impact.

The sentry tower was similarly made. Guards kept watch on the surrounding countryside through small, square windows. It was to one of these windows that Colonel Reynolds stepped at the bidding of McKinn. "I don't see anything," he commented, scouring the ground below.

"Look a little farther out, sir. Just across the road," Sergeant McKinn advised. Having been the second one to see it, he could well understand why the commander put a hand on the wall and shut his eyes for a few moments.

"Bring it in, Sergeant," Colonel Reynolds directed. And then, out of petty spite over the failure of the scouts to locate the renegades, he added, "Go along, Captain. Cover him."

"Me, sir?" Parmalee said in surprise. It was well known that he rarely left the fort, and he liked to think that he had a good excuse. For one thing, his presence was seldom required in the field. His job consisted of sitting behind his desk and issuing orders to the Apaches who volunteered to serve as scouts against their own kind. Which suited him just fine. The thought of going up against a band of renegades terrified him half to death. In his office he was safe, or as safe as any soldier stationed in Arizona could be. "Shouldn't Private Gibbs go?"

Reynolds turned. "I want you to," he said sternly. "So hop to it."

Parmalee broke out in a cold sweat the moment his hands touched the ladder. At the gate, he drew his revolver and cocked it. He thought he noticed a twinkle in the noncom's eyes, a twinkle put there at his expense, but the sergeant was too canny to be obvious. "Open up," Parmalee barked at the four privates awaiting word.

For some reason the sun seemed hotter outside the walls than it had inside, but Parmalee chalked the feeling up to his imagination. He glued himself to the noncom's heels, his eyes darting in every direction.

The ground near the fort had been cleared of most vegetation and anything else hostiles could hide behind. But across the road the chaparral was thick enough to conceal an army. Mesquite and shindaggers predominated, plants that tore mercilessly into unwary horses and men.

Yet Apaches, as Capt. Paramlee knew, navigated mesquite forests with ease. He was sure that unseen eyes were on him as he crossed the dusty road to a low bank. So intent was he on spotting hidden warriors that he forgot all about the memento left by the renegades until he stood right in front of it. His stomach churned at the sight, and he thought he would be sick.

The severed human head of a white man had been impaled on a sharp stake. His eyes had been gouged out, his tongue hacked off. His mouth hung wide open, locked in his death scream.

"Sweet Jesus," Sergeant McKinn breathed. "It's Jim!"

Parmalee looked again and recognized the distorted features of Cpl. Ralston, a likeable cuss whose only failing was his cocky attitude. They had talked a few times over drinks, and it had been Paramlee's opinion that the young trooper failed to give the Apaches their due as fighters. "Given half a chance," the corporal had bragged, "I can hold my own anywhere, any time. Apaches don't scare me as much as they do the rest of you."

Now, staring down at the grisly handiwork of the renegades, Parmalee shook his head and said under his breath, "They should have."

Sergeant McKinn, about to wrest the stake free, looked up. "What was that, sir?"

"Nothing. Proceed."

McKinn choked back the bitter bile that rose in his throat, gripped the stake in both brawny hands, and yanked. The stake was looser than he had figured, and it shot up, the head bumping into his face. He inhaled the foul odor of sweat and something much worse.

Holding the hideous object at arm's length, McKinn hurried toward the gate. He was worried, but not about Apaches. Of more concern was whether anyone had seen him talking to Jim Ralston shortly before the corporal left the fort to go after the White Apache. He wouldn't want the colonel to suspect that he had been a party to Ralston's hunt, if only indirectly.

McKinn kept close tabs on the men under him. It was his duty to see that they were in a constant state of battle-readiness, to insure that morale and performance were at high levels. So he pried, he snooped, he spied on troopers if need be, all to insure that the cogs of the military machine ran as smoothly as they were supposed to.

It had been plain that Corporal Ralston had been up to something. The man had taken a furlough but let it be known he was staying in Arizona instead of going back East to visit his kin. That alone had aroused McKinn's suspicions. Then, when he learned Ralston had bought camping supplies and finagled the loan of a mule, he had taken it on himself to confront his subordinate.

Ralston had admitted he was going after Clay Taggart. Right then and there McKinn should have marched him over to the colonel's office and reported it, but McKinn had turned his back and let Ralston ride off. He still had the forty dollars Ralston had given him, that and the now empty promise of another three-hundred once Ralston received the bounty.

Col. Reynolds waited at the gate. He avoided

staring at the head again, and asked, "Any idea who it is this time?" Sgt. McKinn told him.

The commanding officer sighed, feeling suddenly older than his years and very, very tired. "This can't go on," he said bleakly. "The bastard is rubbing our noses in our own incompetence. Once word spreads, even the tame Indians will be laughing at us behind our backs. More young hotheads are bound to join the renegades, thinking they can do so with impunity."

"What would you suggest we do, sir?" Capt. Parmalee said, not really caring one way or the other just so long as it didn't involve his leaving the security of the fort. "We've increased patrols. We've sent our best scouts deep into the mountains time and again. All with no result."

Sgt. McKinn added his two cents worth, inspired by the three-hundred dollars he would never see. "It's too bad the Chiricahuas aren't as fond of money as we are, sir. If they were, we might be able to pay a turncoat to lead us to the White Apache's lair."

Col. Reynolds glanced sharply at the noncom. A strange expression came over him and he smiled broadly. "Sergeant, I do believe that you're a genius."

"Me, sir?"

"Find Capt. Forester and Lt. Peterson. I want them in my office within half an hour. You too, Parmalee."

Parmalee didn't like being included, but objecting was out of the question. "You sound excited, sir. Mind filling me in?"

The commander swiveled on a boot heel. "In due time, Captain. All you need to know for now is that at long last I've hit on a way of putting an end to the White Apache once and for all."

Blood Treachery

* * *

At that very moment, the man the Army most wanted to eliminate or capture was several miles distant, bearing to the northwest at a tireless dog-trot. His breechcloth and long black hair swayed as he ran. The burning sun warmed his bronzed back and limbs, but not to the point of giving him heatstroke, as it might have done once.

There were times when Clay Taggart marveled at the changes he had undergone. Before hooking up with Delgadito, he had never gone anywhere unless it was on horseback. And he never, ever ventured into the wilderness unless he had a water skin or a canteen along.

Now look at him, Clay mused. He was more Apache than white. Like those whose ways he had adopted, he could run half a day without tiring. A single swallow of water could last him for many hours. One meal every twenty-four hours was all he needed. And he could live off the land better than any white man in the whole Territory. His own mother, if she were still alive, wouldn't recognize him if he were to walk right up to her.

He was an Apache, by choice. Lickoyee-shis-inday, they called him. White Man Of The Woods. The only white-eye ever to be so honored. And Clay was honored.

There had been a time, back when Clay made his living as a rancher, that he'd regarded all Apaches as vermin, fit only to be wiped out to the last man, woman, and child. His attitude had been typical of most whites who lived in the Territory. And in a way, even now, he couldn't blame them.

For far too many years the citizens of Arizona had lived with the ever-present threat of Apache raids. Scores of innocent settlers had been

29

ruthlessly butchered. Travelers had been waylaid as regularly as clockwork and slaughtered in horrible fashion. Women and children had been taken captive, never to be seen again. Small wonder the whites hated Apaches, all Apaches. Small wonder the whites wanted the Chiricahuas and every other tribe exterminated.

Sentiments Clay Taggart had strongly shared. Then came the day he had been framed by his wealthy neighbor, Miles Gillett, so Gillett could get his hands on Clay's land. Clay had been forced to flee, had been chased by a posse into the Dragoon Mountains. There they had caught him, strung him up, and left him for dead.

How strangely fate worked, Clay mused. He would have gone to meet his Maker that day had Delgadito not elected to cut him down so he could arrange a truce between the Army and the renegades. A truce that never came to pass.

As a result of circumstances no man could have predicted or prevented, Clay Taggart found himself a member of the most notorious Apache band in the Southwest. He was wanted by the Army and civilian law, and a huge bounty had been placed on his head, dead or alive.

Thanks to Miles Gillett, those who had once called Clay their pard had turned against him. His own kind were out for his blood. One mistake, and his corpse might end up on public display in Tucson, where the curious and the timid would come take a peek for a measly twenty-five cents. When the novelty wore off and folks no longer cared, the undertaker would likely as not toss his body out on the desert to be devoured by coyotes.

But Clay wasn't about to let that happen. Not

yet. Not while he had unfinished business to settle with Miles Gillett. One day, soon, he would
launch a raid on Gillett's spread and pay the bastard back for the scar on his neck—and for the
loss of his ranch and the woman he loved.

Suddenly Clay's reverie was shattered by the
feeling that he was no longer alone. Instantly he
halted and crouched, unslinging the Winchester
as he did so. A study of both rims of the gully
along which he was making his way revealed no
hidden enemies.

He reminded himself that he must be extra
vigilant. Being so close to the fort increased the
odds of being spotted by soldiers. Should any
recognize him, they'd be on him like rabid wolves
on a panther, eager to bring him down no matter
what the cost.

Clay saw no one. He reminded himself that
Cuchillo Negro and Ponce were out there somewhere. They had insisted on tagging along on his
trek to Fort Bowie to leave the keepsake. Then
the three of them had split up in case the soldiers
gave chase.

As usual, though, the troopers had not shown
any such desire. He'd watched them for a while,
seen them recover the head of the corporal and
then go on about their daily routine as if nothing
out of the ordinary had taken place.

Before Clay Taggart became the White Apache,
he had been proud of the Army presence in
Arizona, proud of the job the Fifth Cavalry
was doing to keep the Apaches in line. Now
that the shoe was on the other foot, as it were,
White Apache wished they would all pack up and
leave. Most were inept greenhorns, cannon fodder
for glory-seeking politicians in Washington, sent
to protect the frontier but in the process being

duped into serving the ends of a wicked schemer like Miles Gillett.

It was Gillett, Clay had heard, who put up half the blood money for the reward on his head. Gillett who had saturated the area with wanted posters printed at his own expense. To Clay's way of thinking, his enemy was growing desperate to see him dead. He liked to think that Gillett lay in bed at night caked with sweat, unable to sleep for worry over where he would strike next.

Gillett's worry would mount on hearing of the head. It would show Gillett that no one could stop him, that he could go where he wanted when he wanted, with impunity. It would remind Gillett that one day soon he would show up in the middle of the night to claim his vengeance.

White Apache smiled at the image, then shook his head to derail the train of thought. He had to stay alert. It was another ten miles to the spot where he would reunite with Cuchillo Negro and Ponce. He had better be on his way.

Rising, he took but a few steps when somewhere up ahead a rifle cracked. Almost at the selfsame instant, an invisible hammer slammed into the side of his head.

Chapter Three

It happened so fast that Taggart was on his side on the ground with blood seeping from his temple before he quite realized someone had shot at him. Dazed, White Apache rolled onto his back and fought a rising tide of darkness that tried to engulf him. Giving in to the veil would doom him, because whoever had ambushed him would move in close to finish the job.

Forcing his arms and legs to move, White Apache pushed up into a crouch and closer to the left wall of the gully so he would be harder to hit. No other shots rang out, which indicated the bushwhacker had lost sight of him when he fell. It also meant the man was somewhere above the gully, secreted in the heavy brush bordering it.

Clay's senses reached out and probed the manzanita, as would a true Apache's. His posture mimicked that of a coiled warrior. Even the set of his mind was like that of a genuine

Chiricahua, devoted to one thought and only one: killing whoever had tried to kill him.

Clay Taggart truly lived up to his new name as he glided forward parallel to the left-hand rim. His moccasins made no noise when he placed them down. Soundless as a ghost, the hunted had now become the hunter. He had his thumb on the rifle hammer, his forefinger curved lightly around the trigger.

Suddenly White Apache heard the faintest of noises from the manzanita on the right side of the gully. Sturdy legs pumping, he went up the gradual incline in a rush, streaked over the lip, and dashed in among the shrub-like trees, which only grew to a height of five or six feet. Stopping behind a bush, White Apache did as Delgadito had taught him: he bent his body to imitate the shape of the bush. Anyone seeing his outline would mistake him for the plant's shadow.

From under narrowed eyelids, White Apache sought evidence of the ambusher. He assumed it to be a white man and was supremely confident he would spot the culprit before too long. Time went by, however, and White Apache spied no one, nor did he hear the whisper of footsteps. Whoever lurked out there was highly skilled. Maybe, he reasoned, it was one of the Apache scouts working for the Army.

Five minutes became ten. Ten became twelve. White Apache straightened and moved off, using every available bit of cover, blending into the background as expertly as would a real Chiricahua. Despite that, the ambusher caught sight of him.

White Apache was just about to dart from one manzanita to another when the bark of the one he was standing behind erupted in a spray of slivers that stung his cheek and nearly took out an eye. He dropped, relying on the gunshot to pinpoint the position of the one who wanted to kill him. It came from dense growth about twenty-five yards away.

Going to ground, White Apache scrutinized the wall of vegetation from top to bottom. Thanks to the training of the Apaches, he could ferret out a mouse at that distance, but try as he might, he couldn't find the rifleman.

It was baffling. White Apache considered himself the equal of any man in Arizona, white or red. Yet whoever wanted to rub him out was proving to be more than a match for him.

Crawling slowly, White Apache angled to the right in a wide loop that brought him to the rear of the stand where the killer was hidden. Parting high stems of grass, he had an unobstructed view, but still he saw no one.

Someone saw him.

Again a rifle banged, twice this time, and at each shot the dirt under White Apache's chin flew into the air, some getting into his mouth. He rolled to the left and kept on rolling until he was well camouflaged. Then, snaking along on his side, he moved a dozen yards to the west.

By this time White Apache's temple pulsed with pounding pain. He touched the wound and discovered the blood flow had stopped. By a sheer fluke he had been spared. Another quarter of an inch to the right, however, and the bushwhacker would have put a window in his skull.

White Apache moved behind a small boulder. It occurred to him that his unseen adversary might be playing him for a fool. The man could be trying to pin him down until a patrol arrived. As good as White Apache was, eluding over thirty mounted men while on foot would tax him to his limits.

Deciding that he would rather live to fight another day than to stay and possibly be overwhelmed, White Apache crept off to the northwest. When he had put enough ground behind him, he broke into a trot, ignoring the anguish that racked his head. The wound was swelling, a bad sign. As every frontiersman worthy of the name knew, more victims of gunshot wounds died from infections that set in after the fact than from the actual shots. He had to dress his as soon as possible.

To the north, a day's journey, lay a ribbon of a stream known only to the Apaches. White Apache bent his steps toward it and kept on the lookout for certain plants used by Chiricahua women to treat gunshots. The next second, without warning, White Apache caught sight of a figure in the underbrush in front of him. He promptly halted and brought the Winchester to his shoulder.

The figure was big but sped along with surprising speed, the flow of his movements betraying Indian lineage. As if the warrior sensed he was being watched, he abruptly stopped and spun. White Apache glimpsed features set in a mask of hatred, features he felt he should recognize but didn't. He fixed a hasty bead, then fired. Simultaneously, the figure dropped and snapped off two shots of his own, which were too high.

Diving flat, White Apache wriggled to a pipe-organ cactus. Another shot rang out and a section of the plant inches from his face blew apart. He scrambled onward, under a paloverde over ten feet high. Here, for the time being, he was safe.

After working the lever of his rifle to feed a new round into the chamber, White Apache slid around the paloverde into dry weeds. Here he exercised greater caution, since the stems were prone to rustle and rattle at the least little pressure.

His hunch about the bushwhacker being an Indian had proven correct, but he didn't know what to make of the warrior's behavior. Why try to kill him, then run off when he was hurt and at a disadvantage? Yet that was exactly what the man must have done, heading north from the gully minutes before he did, perhaps bound for the same stream.

It was a puzzle worthy of attention, later. For the moment White Apache had to devote himself to staying alive. He tested the sluggish breeze with his ears and his nose but neither revealed the warrior's location. Picking up a stone, he hefted it a few times, then pitched it as far as he could to one side. It clattered as it fell into the brush, spooking a pair of doves that took wing side by side. But it didn't do as he had hoped and lure the warrior into the open.

The pain in his head was growing worse. White Apache decided to take the fight to his foe and made straight for the spot where he had last seen the figure. He came on tracks, which were small given the size of their maker, leading off to the west. Once again the ambusher had fled.

Or was it even the same man? White Apache wondered. Maybe he had stumbled on a different warrior and mistaken him for the dry-gulcher. But if that was the case, why had the man's features lit with hatred on seeing him? Had it been a Pima or a Maricopa, traditional enemies of the Apaches?

There were plenty of questions and too few answers. White Apache stood and resumed his interrupted trek. He had to steel himself against

37

the rising agony in his head, which was making it hard for him to think clearly. All he needed was some nice, cool water, he told himself. Once he reached the stream and dressed the wound, everything would be fine. It had to be.

He refused to die until Miles Gillett had paid for making an outcast of him.

From a patch of mesquite more than 100 yards off, a pair of beady dark eyes, simmering with raw spite, watched Lickoyee-shis-inday depart.

The eyes were set under thick beetling brows in a huge moon of a face belonging to Palacio, leader of the Chiricahuas. A rarity among Apaches, Palacio had the distinction of being the only fat warrior in the tribe. Yet when he moved, as he did now in trotting briskly to the southeast, his body showed a supple grace and hinted at latent strength that belied his bulk.

In the white man's world, Palacio would be considered a dandy. A yellow headband kept his black hair in place. He wore a bright red shirt and leggings decorated with blue and red beads. His moccasins were beaded, as was the sheath of his long hunting knife. Palacio dressed as he did because unlike the majority of his people he had a constant hankering for the finer things life had to offer. Good food, and lots of it. Colorful clothes such as the whites and *Nakai-yes* wore. Fine horses and guns. These were what mattered, in Palacio's estimation.

He had not always been that way. As a little boy, he had been just like his childhood friends. Many a day had been spent prowling the mountains dressed in a leather breechcloth, many a night huddled next to a campfire listening to the tales told by the elders of the tribe. Then

Blood Treachery

Mexicans seeking copper came to Chiricahua country. The *Nakai-yes,* they were called. And these Mexicans brought with them all manner of new possessions.

Palacio had been dazzled witless by the wealth of these smiling strangers. His father, a revered chief, had taken him time and again to visit Santa Rita del Cobre. He had seen *Nakai-yes* wearing pistols that shone like the sun and carrying rifles that killed men at distances unheard of before. He had eaten meals so rich and sweet and sometimes deliriously hot that afterward he had lain on the ground like a contented camp dog and savored the sensation.

Those were days Palacio recollected fondly. His father had been friendly to the *Nakai-yes,* and Palacio had followed in his footsteps when he assumed the mantle of leadership.

Much later the Americans came, and Palacio had been one of the few who advocated greeting them with open arms. But the people had listened to those who counseled war, and as a result the Chiricahuas were now confined to a reservation. Many remembered his earlier guidance, though, and his esteem had risen steadily to where Palacio was now the single most influential warrior in the whole tribe. His people did nothing without first consulting him.

There were exceptions. Delgadito had seen fit to break away from the main body and start his own band. Palacio had warned him that doing so was unwise and predicted that so small a band would be easy prey for soldiers from both sides of the border, not to mention the marauding packs of scalp hunters hired by the State of Sonora in Mexico to rid them of Apaches.

Once again Palacio had been proven right.

Delgadito's band had nearly been wiped out. He often regretted that Delgadito had not been among those slain, but such was life. He'd been content with having Delgadito's influence among their people shattered, and he had expected the few survivors to come slinking back into the village with their tails between their legs to admit they had been wrong to resist the whites.

Palacio had dreamed of that day, had dreamed of making Delgadito squirm for defying him. But then along came the so-called White Apache, and to Palacio's annoyance the small band of renegades made a series of successful raids that had stirred up the hotheads in the tribe into thinking that the time must be ripe for rising up against the Americans and driving them from Chiricahua land.

Not long ago Palacio had visited the renegades at one of their many sanctuaries in the mountains. Delgadito had set up the meeting to ask that his band be allowed to slip into the village now and then to visit relatives and friends. The renegades missed them, he had claimed. But Palacio knew better. The real reason Delgadito wanted to return was to persuade others to join his little band, and thereby weaken Palacio's hold on the tribe.

It had given the chief immense joy to refuse—tactfully of course. He had pointed out that the Army and the reservation police were everywhere, and keen to get their hands on the renegades. Should Delgadito's band be captured in the village, it would not sit well with the Americans, who might see fit to make reservation life harder than it already was. The Chiricahuas might be punished for Delgadito's deeds.

Reluctantly, Delgadito had agreed. They had gone their separate ways, and until that very morning Palacio had not set eyes on any of the renegades. Then he had spotted Clay Taggart.

It was safe to say that where Palacio despised Delgadito, he positively hated Lickoyee-shis-inday. It was Taggart who had saved Delgadito from the scalp hunters, Taggart who had gone on to lead a successful raid into Mexico and against several ranchers, Taggart who was now the most feared man on the frontier. Because of his reputation, many younger warriors were seriously thinking about joining the renegades.

The White Apache was a genuine threat to Palacio's leadership. Accordingly, Palacio would give anything to have the white-eye eliminated. How could he pass up the chance?

There Palacio had been, on his way northward to meet a pair of smugglers who brought him special items from time to time in exchange for gold nuggets, when he had seen White Apache enter a gully. It had been easy for Palacio to shadow him and wait for the right moment to take his life. Unfortunately, once again the white-eye's astounding luck protected him. Palacio, who could put out the eye of a squirrel at fifty yards, had merely nicked Clay Taggart.

It surprised Palacio that the White Apache had been able to track him northward from the gully. Despite his size, he was as adept as any of his people at leaving few tracks and disguising those he did make. He thought he had given the American the slip, and yet had he not turned at just the right moment to check his back trail, Lickoyee-shis-inday would have put a bullet into him.

Palacio was beginning to understand why White Apache was so widely dreaded. The man had an amazing knack for death and destruction. Not many moons ago, he had witnessed a formal fight between the white-eye and one of the most skilled knife fighters in the tribe and been stunned when White Apache won.

All of which confirmed Palacio's resolve to have the man disposed of. The only question was how to go about it. He wasn't about to try again himself. And none of the Chiricahuas were going to jeopardize their lives without ample cause.

Palacio jogged on under the hot sun. His meeting with the smugglers would have to take place another day. The White Apache had been heading northward too, and Palacio didn't care to run the risk of encountering the man again. Better by far to return to the village and have one of his two wives tend to his growling belly. Several helpings of the spicy bean dish so favored by the *Nakai-yes* would do wonders for his disposition. That, and five or six gourds of *tizwin*.

A leader had to keep his priorities straight or he was no leader at all.

It was shortly before sunset when Palacio heard the drum of hoofs and jingle of cavalry accoutrements. He set down the heady *tizwin* he had been drinking and nodded at his younger wife, who dutifully moved to the wickiup entrance.

"Four *soldados*," she reported. "White Hair leads them. Another is the *capitan* who killed Chivari. And Klo-sen trails behind."

This was most unexpected. White Hair was the Chiricahua name for Colonel Reynolds, the commander of Fort Bowie. The captain she spoke of was Gerald Forester, one of the few officers who had taken the time to learn some of the Apache tongue. And Klo-sen was an Army scout, a Mescalero but still Apache. For them to pay him a visit without first letting him know they were coming was most unusual.

"I will greet them outside," Palacio said, heaving erect. "Bring my pipe and tobacco pouch."

Lumbering outdoors, Palacio sank into a large chair he had obtained at the trading post. All around him was other evidence of his wealth. His wickiup was the only one in the village that sported canvas sides instead of being made from brush and grass. Nearby were three metal pails rather than earthen jugs. A metal pot containing cooking utensils sat by the entrance. And leaning against the side of the lodge was a new shovel.

The riders were twenty yards off. Men and animals were caked with dust, except for the Mescalero who somehow managed to look as if he had just come from his own lodge.

Palacio swelled out his chest and leaned back, his pudgy hands folded in his ample lap. It pleased him immensely to note that many of his people were on hand to witness the event. Here was the chief white-eye from the gigantic stone lodge paying him, Palacio, a visit. It would confirm the story he had been spreading that his council was widely esteemed by the whites, and that the white-eyes looked to him first when dealing with the Chiricahuas.

Clearing his throat, Palacio called out in near perfect English, "Greetings, Colonel. You honor my wickiup with your presence." He had made it a point to learn the tongue of the Americans, just as he had learned the tongue of the Mexicans before them. It was a gift of the *gans,* this ability to learn new tongues easily. The last Chiricahua to have the gift was Cochise, who had risen to be a legend among his people in his own time. Could Palacio do any less?

Col. Reynolds raised a hand in salute and reined up. The ride from Fort Bowie had been long and hot, and he had made matters worse by pushing the horses to insure he would arrive well before dark. Removing his hat, he plucked a monogrammed handkerchief from a pocket and wiped his face as best he was able to make himself presentable.

Sgt. McKinn was the first to dismount. He handed the reins of his horse to Klo-sen and hurried to hold the commander's horse.

Looking on, Capt. Vincent Paramalee smirked. In his eyes, McKinn was only sucking up to the colonel, a detestable act Parmalee would never commit. He licked his dry lips, thought of the flask secreted in his saddlebags, and wished with all his might that he could take a swig.

Capt. Gerald Forester swung down and let his reins drop to the ground. He made no attempt to improve his appearance, nor did his thirst show. Forester was a veteran of the Indians Wars, first in the Dakotas and for the past four years in Arizona. He could live off the land, spoke fluent Apache, and had patrolled the Territory from east to west, north to south. To put it succinctly, he was the most experienced officer in the Fifth Cavalry. It was a fact of which Col. Reynolds was well aware, and why he had brought Forester along. Of all his subordinates, Reynolds relied on Forester's judgment the most.

Palacio also knew the captain's reputation, and didn't like him. It was Forester, after all, who had tracked down and slain the renegade Chivari in personal combat over three winters ago. But Palacio's dislike stemmed more from the impression he had that Forester didn't think very highly of him than from the death of Chivari, who had always been a minor thorn in Palacio's side.

Klo-sen was the only one who stayed on his horse, a rifle slanted across his thighs. While he shared kinship to the Chiricahuas in that they were all Apaches, there had been a time long ago when Mescaleros and Chiricahuas fought against one another. He no more trusted them than he would Comanches.

"Hello again, Palacio," Colonel Reynolds said, advancing and offering his hand. "I'm glad you're here. I was afraid we'd travel all this way and miss you."

The Chiricahua chief shook. Palacio never had fully understood the silly white custom of touching hands, but he did it anyway to make them happy. "My heart is glad to see you again, my friend," he said solemnly. "Raven Wing is bringing my pipe. We will smoke, then talk over what brings you to my people." He emphasized the last few words.

Reynolds would much rather have gotten straight to the point, but he had visited the chief before and knew that failure to smoke might be taken as an insult. So he sat cross-legged with his subordinates and Palacio in a circle in front of the canvas wickiup and passed the lit pipe around. Palacio then raised the pipe to the heavens, shifted, and handed it Raven Beak.

"Now then, White Hair," Palacio said. "To what do I owe the pleasure of your visit?"

"Desperation," Col. Reynolds said. "I want to stop the White Apache once and for all."

"We share the same dream," Palacio said, his countenance clouding. "But we have tried many times and he is still alive."

"I have a new idea," Reynolds said. "I want to make one of your people very, very rich."

"Rich?"

"Yes. Do you think any of them would like to own eight new horses, forty new blankets, six new knives, an ax, and all the tobacco they can carry?"

The vision of so much wealth made Palacio's head spin. "Who would not?"

"Excellent. All those things will be given to the warrior who tells me where White Apache and Delgadito are hiding. And as a bonus, if the information leads to the deaths of the renegades, I'll throw in fifty dollars worth of credit at the trading post."

Palacio had to bite his lip to keep from howling for sheer joy. "Never fear, White Hair. The renegades are as good as dead."

Chapter Four

It was strange to have one's head feel as if it were an overripe melon.

Clay Taggart, the White Apache, staggered on through the darkness feeling just that way. His head pounded with every heartbeat. It had swelled horribly during the long hours he had been on the trail, and merely placing a finger on his temple provoked spasms so intense he could barely stand. If he were to trip and strike his head, he was sure he would never get up again.

All these factors made the decision to press on through the night the only logical one to make. White Apache needed to reach water as quickly as possible. Any delay, even a night's rest, might weaken him to the point where he would be unable to go on.

About midnight, White Apache had begun to feel oddly sluggish, and a distinct mineral taste filled his mouth. He had no idea what to make of it, but it did not bode well. Now the time was close to four in the morning and in another hour the eastern horizon would streak with pale harbingers of dawn. And still he had not reached the stream.

White Apache paused and studied the landscape to get his bearings. Even at the plodding pace he had maintained for the past six hours, he should have struck the stream by now. Either he had strayed off course or the stream had gone dry, which many did in Arizona during the hotter months of the year. But this one was supposed to run year-round.

It should be there.

He tried to lick his lips but his tongue was as swollen as his head. Slinging the Winchester over a shoulder, he cradled his chin in his hands, holding his head steady so he could think a little more clearly.

The landmarks, such as they were, weren't familiar. To the northwest dark peaks reared. To the northeast grew heavy timber. All around him lay dry land dotted with boulders.

There should be grass, Clay remembered. If he was close to the stream he would come on a quarter-mile strip of grass grazed by deer and antelope.

Goading his legs into motion, White Apache tramped northward, using the North Star to steer his course. It was yet another of the many tricks Delgadito had taught him, lessons that had already saved his hide more than once.

Reminisces of the renegade leader occupied him for a while. He thought of all they had been through, of the times Delgadito had pulled his bacon out of the fire, of the enemies they had faced and beaten. He considered Delgadito a pard in every sense of the word, although of late he had grown to suspect that Delgadito was using him in some manner to regain his lost standing in the tribe.

So what if he was? That was Clay's attitude. He owed Delgadito a debt he could never repay, which made it only fair for him to help the warrior become a leader again.

One thing was for sure. No matter how many successful raids Clay led, no matter how many whites or *Nakai-yes* he slew, or how much plunder he took, the Chiricahuas would never accept him as a leader because of his heritage. In the entire history of the tribe only full-blooded Chiricahuas had held such posts.

That was all right, too, in Clay's book. He had no desire to become a war chief. He had no urge to lead. His sole motivation for living was sweet and simple: revenge.

The next moment White Apache stepped on a stone that shot from under his foot and caused his leg to swing out in front of him. He tried to regain his footing, but in his condition it was like asking a drunk to walk a straight line. Down he went, hard, onto his back.

The pounding became thunder. The number of stars in the firmament doubled. He heard a low groan and realized the sound came from his throat. Racked by pain, he nearly blacked out.

For the longest while Clay lay there, his eyes closed, waiting for the torment to subside so he could go on. The wind stirred his hair and whistled among the boulders. He dozed off, briefly.

The patter of stealthy footfalls brought White Apache around. Ears pricked, he listened as the sound came closer and closer. Cracking his eyes, he spied a ghostly shape crouched about fifteen feet away.

Painter! Clay's mind screeched. Some called them panthers, some mountain lions, others cougars. However they were called, they infested the Southwest and were most numerous in the border country. Although normally they fought shy of humans, there had been occasions when bolder cats had pounced on people.

Girding himself, White Apache sat up and placed a hand on his pistol. At close range, at night, it was the better gun to use. He would be able to get off more shots, faster.

Normally, anyway. Tonight White Apache could barely lift the six-shooter and level the barrel. He saw the lion slink closer, crouched as if to spring, attracted, no doubt, by the stale scent of blood.

It was a gigantic animal. He had heard tales of panthers seven feet long from nose tip to tail's end, but this one was bigger, seven and a half feet if it was an inch. Now the cat growled, rumbling deep in its chest, its serpentine tail whipping like a berserk sidewinder.

To White Apache's dismay, he found that he was unable to hold the revolver steady. His hand shook as if from a conniption. And when he attempted to take aim, he couldn't keep the sight fixed on the panther.

"Damn," Clay said aloud.

Hissing, the mountain lion backed up a few steps.

"Don't like the sound of my voice, do you?" Clay said. "Well, here's something you'll like even less." So saying, he banged off a shot in the predator's general direction.

One moment the panther was there, the next it was gone. Blinking, Clay looked and looked but saw no trace of the beast. He recollected being told once that lions liked to circle around behind their prey so he shifted to glance over a shoulder. The movement triggered a blast of anguish between his ears. A black veil, blacker than the night itself, seemed to sweep toward him from out of the recesses of his own mind and enclosed him in its inky grasp.

White Apache struggled to stay awake, to stay alert. The mountain lion was liable to jump him at any second. But, try as he might, he slipped deeper and deeper into the indigo well. The last thing he felt was his cheek hitting the earth.

There is nothing quite like waking up to find yourself alive when you have every right to believe you should be dead.

White Apache squinted at the blazing sun, which hung low in the eastern sky, and gratefully inhaled the hot air. He slowly rose onto his elbows. The Colt was beside him, the panther nowhere to be seen.

The drumming inside his skull, though, persisted, as bad as ever. Propping his hands under him, he rose, picking up the pistol as he did so. No sooner did he straighten than a wave of dizziness washed over him, threatening to flatten him again. He held himself still until the vertigo passed, then shuffled northward.

Clay was so thirsty he would have dunked his face into a mud puddle to suck the moisture from the mud. He could barely open his mouth, and when he did so, his lips felt as if they were cracking in half.

Delgadito had taught him which cactus plants contained water, but there were none in that area.

51

The few clumps of vegetation he could see would provide no relief at all.

The best White Apache could do was slip a pebble in his mouth to suck on. But when he tried, his swollen tongue prevented him from inserting the pebble past his puffy lips. In annoyance he cast the pebble down. The movement of his arm jarred his head and the pain became almost unbearable. He stumbled, about to pass out again, but by the sheer strength of his willpower he was able to plod on, weak and weary and closer to death than he had ever been.

White Apache was only vaguely conscious of things around him. He knew the sun was climbing, knew the air was as hot as the scorching inferno of hell, knew when he nearly stepped on a gila monster and had to sidestep or be bitten, knew when, sometime about noon, his legs began to tingle and go numb.

This was the end, White Apache reflected. He had survived being hanged, survived being shot at, survived knife fights and clashes with the cavalry and *federales*, only to die because of an infected wound, lost in the middle of nowhere with no one to mourn his passing, not so much as a single living soul who would shed a single tear or remember him fondly once he was gone.

Dying alone and unmourned had to be one of the most horrible fates to befall a person. He thought of his folks, the only two people who had ever cared for him with their whole hearts.

Lilly certainly hadn't. The woman he had loved more than life itself had betrayed him, had forsaken him for Miles Gillett, had even helped Gillett capture him and done nothing when Gillett's hands had taken a bull whip to him and beaten him within an inch of his life.

Blood Treachery

Now Clay would never get to pay her back. Nor would he ever have the satisfaction of cutting her wicked, treacherous husband into little pieces, or of slowly strangling the bastard to death with his bare hands. Sometimes life could be so damned unfair.

That was the last thought the White Apache had before his legs gave out completely and his head smashed onto the hard earth. For an instant the pain flared and he hurt as he had never hurt before from head to toe.

Then there was nothing.

The face seemed to shimmer and dance above him like a mirage. White Apache attempted to focus, but his thoughts spun as if caught in a whirlpool, mimicking the image. Suddenly the features sharpened. The face became clear, or he believed it did, and he saw above him the lovely features and dark hair of his beloved.

"Lilly!" Clay breathed.

Someone spoke, but it wasn't Lilly's voice. The words were alien, a tongue he didn't know.

"Lilly, is that you?"

The whirlpool slowed to a crawl, then stopped. The shimmer faded, and the face became crystal clear. It was the face of a woman, but not Lilly Gillett. The woman's short hair was darker than Lilly's, as was the hue of her skin. She was an Indian.

White Apache went to rise on his elbows but the woman spoke sharply and held him down by the shoulders. Then a shadow fell over them.

In his delirium, White Apache assumed that the woman was pinning him in place so her man could finish him off. His logic ran thus: Was he not dressed like an Apache? Did he not look like an

Apache warrior in all respects? And wasn't it also true that every tribe in Arizona had a longstanding grudge against the Apaches over years of Apache raids? Therefore it seemed obvious to him that a roving band had found him lying there helpless and were about to rub him out.

The insight roused White Apache into defending himself. Mustering what little strength remained in his limbs, he lashed out, flinging the woman from him so he could sit up. His hand fell to the Colt, which the woman had foolishly left in its holster, and he twisted to confront the source of the shadow.

It was a boy, no more than ten or eleven, holding a water skin. He had frozen in shock in the act of opening it.

White Apache paused, confused. He looked for warriors but there were none, just a pair of small bundles lying a few yards away.

The woman had risen to her knees and was regarding him frankly, with no hint of fear in her pretty eyes. She put her warm palm on his chest and said in heavily accented English: "Please. Lie down. We help."

To hear English issuing from her rosy lips was enough to convince White Apache that he was imagining the whole incident. The wound and the sunstroke had taken their toll. His blood had become so poisoned that now he was hallucinating. "You're not real," he blurted thickly, hardly able to form the words. "This is a dream."

The woman beckoned the boy. When he just stood there, too scared to move, she spoke sternly in her own tongue and he handed the water skin over. She removed the stopper.

White Apache felt her press the smooth bag to

54

his lips, felt cool, delicious water trickle into his mouth, around his tongue and down his throat. It was the best water he had ever drunk, without exception. He swallowed, and thought his throat had ruptured. Unexpectedly gagging, he doubled over and came close to retching.

The woman squeezed his arm in reassurance. "Drink slow," she said in her sweetly lilting voice. "Make much sick if don't."

"Who—?" White Apache tried to ask, rasping the question between clenched teeth.

"Later talk. Now try drink."

Gradually the heaves went away. White Apache sat back up and the woman tried again, pouring with infinite care. He was able to swallow this time, and bit by bit the awful ache in his throat disappeared. He could move his tongue a little, even though it felt as if it were still swollen as thick as his wrist.

The woman was patient with him. Again and again she raised the water skin when he nodded, lowered it after a few sips.

By all rights White Apache should have been more interested in the water than in her, but oddly enough he couldn't take his mind, or his eyes, off his deliverer. She was short, no more than five and a half feet tall, but nicely shaped, with a full bosom, small hands, and even white teeth. She wore a loose-fitting top and a wrap-around skirt that clung to her in all the right places, accentuating her curves. Her body smelled of mint.

It had been a long time since Clay Taggart had lain with a woman. Too long. At night he often tossed and turned, dreaming of Lilly, of the rapturous silken glory of her sleek naked body snuggled next to his. Frequently of late, in the mornings he would awaken aroused and frustrated.

Clay wanted a woman of his own, but whenever the notion struck him he discarded it as downright foolish. He was an outlaw, an outcast without a home, wanted by white and red men alike, a price on his head high enough to interest every bounty hunter who lived. Taking a woman into his life would doom her to certain death.

Then there was the matter of Lilly Gillett. Although she had betrayed his trust and perverted their love, Clay still cherished her in his heart of hearts. She had been his first true love, and he figured on treasuring the memory of their time together for as long as he lived.

It was strange, Clay often mused, that a man could love a woman so passionately and hate her so intensely at the same time. How was that possible? Love and hate were opposites. They should cancel one another out. Yet, in some bizarre way, he felt both emotions for Lilly. It came from being addlepated, he reckoned.

The woman shook the water skin, frowned, and capped it. "Little left," she said. "Must save. Very sorry."

"Don't be," Clay croaked. "You saved my life. Who are you? What are you doing in these parts?"

"I am *Ma-ris-ta*. My son, *Col-let-to*. We be Pimas."

"Marista," Clay repeated her name. He had never met a Pima before, but knew of them.

A number of tribes lived in dangerously close proximity to Apache territory. One of the largest were the Pimas, farmers who grew beans, squash, and pumpkins. They lived in round, flat-topped dwellings built with grass and earth, and they were as peaceful as could be. Never once, to Clay's knowledge, had they attacked whites or Mexicans.

Even so, the Pimas were fierce in defense of their land and loved ones, as many Apache, Mohave, and Yuma raiders had found out to their dismay. The Chiricahuas regarded the Pimas as good fighters but looked down their noses at them on general principle; to the Apache way of thinking, anyone who tilled the soil for a living was beneath contempt.

Clay studied the woman and the boy. He wanted to ask a lot more questions but his mouth and throat hurt too much. Pointing to the north, he asked, "Do you know of a stream close by?"

"No," Marista said. "Country new. We lost. Little water." She tapped the water skin.

It dawned on Clay that the mother and son had sacrificed most of what little they had to save him. "Come with me," he suggested. "We'll find more together."

Marista bit her lower lip, her brow knit. The glance she bestowed on Colleto told why.

"I would never harm you," Clay declared. "I'm in your debt, and a Taggart never forgets an obligation."

There was hardly any hesitation on her part. "We come. I help you."

Before Clay could object, the Pima woman had a sturdy arm looped under his shoulder and was hoisting him off the ground. He was going to tell her not to bother, to assure her that he could manage by himself, but his legs put the lie to his claim by buckling. She strained, as the corded muscles of her neck testified, and held him upright.

"Go slow," Marista said, catching his eye. "Your name be?"

"Clay Taggart," he disclosed, and was on the verge of adding that he was also known as Lickoyee-shis-inday when he changed his mind. There wasn't a person in Arizona, white or red, who hadn't heard of the White Apache by now. And since a hefty reward was being offered for his head, dead or alive, he decided it was prudent to keep quiet.

"You dress like Apache," the woman noted. "You part Apache?"

"No," Clay said, and gestured for her to start walking. "Let's head on out. I'm a mite paper-backed at the moment, and I don't rightly know how much longer I can hold out."

Colletto fell in step behind them as Clay and Marista hiked northward. Neither the boy nor his mother carried weapons, which surprised Clay greatly. What could they be thinking, traipsing across the Chiricahua reservation unarmed the way they were doing? Could it be that they had no idea where they were? He set his questions aside for the time being and pushed himself as hard as he dared.

A snail could have gone faster. Or such was Clay's opinion after fifteen minutes had gone by. His legs felt as if they weighed tons. He was so weak that he couldn't lift his feet more than a few inches with each step.

An hour elapsed. Clay had to shake himself a few times to stay on his toes, and each time provoked new stirrings of acute agony. Once the woman halted and gestured for her son to bring the water skin to him but Clay shook his head and said firmly, "No. We'll save it for later in case we need it."

"You need now," Marista noted.

"No. Keep going."

Reluctantly, the Pima obeyed.

Clay shut the misery from his mind and stumbled along at her side. Up close, he could see tiny wrinkles at the corners of her eyes and mouth and noted that her skirt and top were worn and faded. Her sandals were close to falling apart; one had a cracked strap and flapped when she walked. Clearly she had fallen on very hard times. "Where's your husband? Did something happen to him?" he asked at one point.

"Too hot talk now," she said stiffly.

Clay posed no more questions for a while. As the afternoon waxed, the heat climbed. When it was at its worst, he indicated some mesquite off to one side and suggested, "Let's rest in the shade a spell."

Mother and son sat a few feet from him, her arm around the boy's shoulders. She had a large pouch slung over her shoulder, the only possession she owned other than the water skin.

"Do you have any food?" Clay inquired.

"We did." Marista opened the flap and held the pouch at arm's length so he could see it was empty. "Ate all last sleep."

"If I was fit, I'd rustle you up some grub in two shakes of a calf's tail," Clay said. "As things stand, we'll have to hold out until evening. If we can find the damn stream, there's bound to be plenty of game nearby." He patted the Winchester. "One shot, and we'll gorge on venison until it comes out our ears."

"Out our ears?" Marista said quizzically, placing a hand on one of hers.

Clay chuckled, then winced. "That's what they call a figure of speech. Words which don't make a whole hell of a lot of sense, but folks use them all the time anyway."

"I not understand."

"Doesn't matter. It's not important."

They sat in silence for twenty minutes. Clay's eyelids drooped and his chin bobbed several times but he refused to fall asleep, to appear weak in front of the woman. He found himself admiring her on the sly and being impressed by her bearing and composure.

At length they pressed on. The boy assumed the lead, the water skin slung over his shoulder.

More and more mesquite appeared. Through it wound a game trail bearing deer tracks not more than a day old. Clay became encouraged and kept craning his neck to see what lay ahead. He was the first to spot a tract of waving grass.

As they emerged from the mesquite, the boy jumped up and down and flapped his arms while jabbering excitedly in the Pima tongue. The stream glistened like a sparkling emerald necklace a hundred yards off, flanked by trees.

Clay lurched into a hobbling run, heedless of the consequences, and Marista kept pace. They were both nearly spent when they halted under the limbs of a cottonwood. Colletto, who had dashed on ahead, stood stone still at the water's edge. He had good cause.

From out of a high clump of bushes had stepped two grungy men in grimy buckskins, both armed with rifles. The taller of the pair chortled and exclaimed, "Why, lookee here, Zeb. We're goin' to have us some fun!"

Chapter Five

"*Lickoyee-shis-inday* should have been here by now."

Cuchillo Negro, he whose name meant Black Knife, heard the statement of his young friend but chose to make no comment. The young were always too impatient, and too prone to remark on the obvious when no remark was needed. He knew White Apache was late, but he would not waste breath complaining. It was not the Chiricahua way.

Ponce jumped onto a boulder to scan the canyon below. "We would see him if he were coming. Something must have happened to him."

"What would you have us do?" Cuchillo Negro asked. Not because he needed advice, since he already knew what their next step would be. He asked to test the younger warrior, to gauge whether Ponce had what it took to one day be a warrior of high standing in the tribe.

"We could try to find him," Ponce said, "but it would take us a long time, and in a short while the sun will go down." He swiveled to the northwest. "We would not be able to rejoin Delgadito and Fiero tomorrow morning as we said we would. They will wonder what has happened to us."

"What would White Apache or Delgadito do in such a case?" Cuchillo Negro asked. Using the example set by seasoned warriors to instruct the young was a time-honored Apache custom. How well he remembered his own upbringing, when his father and uncles had taken him under their wing and imparted important lessons that had saved his life many times over.

Ponce, though, had no father, no uncles. The young warrior had lost most of his relatives that terrible day the scalphunters had attacked without warning, slaughtering almost all those who had chosen to follow Delgadito. Only a handful of warriors had escaped, and Delgadito himself would have died had White Apache not whisked him from under the noses of the butchers.

White Apache. Now there was a mystery Cuchillo Negro had yet to unravel. When Delgadito saved the white-eye from being hanged, it had been Delgadito's intent to have the man called Taggart set up a meeting between the cavalry and the renegades. Delgadito's band had grown tired of always being on the run. They'd wanted to return to the reservation, to be among their own people again. Then along came the scalphunters, and changed everything.

Delgadito lost all his influence. He was bad medicine, the reservation Chiricahuas claimed. But never one to give up, Delgadito had seen a way to exploit the white-eye, to use Taggart to regain his lost prestige. And now?

Cuchillo Negro heard Ponce speak and turned. "I think we should split up. One of us should go after White Apache while the other goes on to let Delgadito know what has happened."

The stripling had chosen wisely. Cuchillo Negro was pleased. "You go on. I will track down White Apache." Cuchillo Negro rose and stepped off the flat rock on which he had been perched.

"This very moment?" Ponce asked.

"You would have us wait until morning?"

Ponce made no reply. He knew he had spoken thoughtlessly. To explain would compound his mistake. Hitching at his cartridge belt, he spun and ran off up the mountain with the agility of a bighorn.

Cuchillo Negro lingered until the youth was out of sight before he made off to the south-east. By pushing himself, he would reach the spot where the three of them had separated shortly after dark. Tracking at night was difficult but it could be done, so he would keep going and hope *Lickoyee-shis-inday* was all right.

The Chiricahuas needed him, more than the man knew or would ever suspect.

Palacio sat toward the rear of his wickiup, resplendent in his finest garb, a new red headband framing his oval face and the warm smile he wore to make his five guests feel at ease. He raked them with a probing stare one more time and asked, "Are there any questions?"

Crusty old Nantanh looked up. "This is bad, this thing you want us to do. Chiricahuas do not help enemies kill Chiricahuas."

Chico grunted. "And since when do Chiricahuas care about how many horses they own? Or how many knives? We live for two things, and two

63

things only." He paused. "To kill without being killed and to steal without being caught."

Palacio had foreseen their argument and he was ready. "The welfare of our people matters, or it should to every Chiricahua worthy of the name. And I say to you that unless the renegades are stopped, hard times will befall our people. Is that what you want?"

"Of course not," Juan Pedro said, "but since the beginning of time, Chiricahua has not turned on Chiricahua. Delgadito might have chosen the wrong path, but he is still one of us, still of our blood, still worthy of our loyalty."

Palacio was unruffled. This, too, he had anticipated. For all their love of being independent, when braced by enemies, Apaches of all kinds banded together to preserve their own. "Does this hold true for *Lickoyee-shis-inday* also?"

"White Apache has sided with Delgadito," Nantanh said.

"But does that make him *Shis-Inday?* Does that entitle him to be treated as we would treat one another? Does that mean we should call him our brother?"

"Delgadito does," Nantanh persisted.

Palacio's smile broadened to cover the resentment simmering inside him. The old warrior might be well past his prime but his mind was as sharp as ever and in councils he was always quick to point out flaws in plans and battle strategies. Convincing him would be a challenge.

"Delgadito is entitled," Palacio said suavely. "From what I hear, this White Apache saved his life. But the White Apache did not save me, or any of you. Why, then, should we let him be the cause of the ruin of our people?" Five heads swung toward him.

"What do you mean, the ruin?" Gian-nah-tah said. "What do you know that we do not?"

Palacio played his part perfectly. Leaning forward to give the idea he was confiding a great secret, he said in a low voice only they could hear, "The *Americanos* have run out of patience. They want this White Apache, and they are willing to do whatever is necessary to get him. My good friend, White Hair, the chief of the soldiers at the stone lodge called Bowie, has told me of their plans so that we can take steps to protect ourselves."

"What plans?" Nantanh asked suspiciously.

"The white-eyes think our people must be sheltering the White Apache. They do not believe me when I tell them we want nothing to do with him. So they intend to send in soldiers, more soldiers than there are blades of grass in the hills, to round us up and move us to San Carlos. They will strip us of our lands and make us farm as do the Pimas and Maricopas."

Old Nantanh was red in the face. "I would like to see them try! Our land was promised to us for as long as the sun and moon exist. Their great chief gave his promise to Cochise. I was there. I heard."

"As did many of us," Palacio said. "But you know how the white-eyes can be. Sometimes they speak with two tongues. Sometimes their great chief says one thing and lesser chiefs say another. In this, though, I think they all speak as one. Unless we do something, our people will suffer."

Indecision etched five faces, and Palacio took advantage.

"White Hair is trying to help us by giving us a chance to help them. If we let them know where to find the White Apache, I have his promise that our people will not be moved to San Carlos." Palacio sat back, smugly confident they would give in. The story about being moved to San Carlos was untrue, a lie he had made to lend weight to his arguments. He knew that for some time there had been rumors the Army intended to relocate the tribe, which the Chiricahuas would do anything to prevent.

Nantanh snorted. "A promise! It is a threat. Unless we give in, we will be punished." He shook a bony fist in the air. "If Cochise were still alive the white-eyes would not treat us as they do!"

"No one wishes Cochise were still with us more than I do," Palacio claimed. The reality was that he had been overjoyed when the venerable chief passed on. Cochise had never liked him, had relegated him to a minor role in the peace talks and shunned him whenever possible.

Chico spoke next. "I have no objection to helping the soldiers find the White Apache but I will not betray Delgadito. He is my friend."

"Mine too," Juan Pedro said.

Palacio saw his grand scheme unraveling before his eyes. "How many times must I tell you? It is White Apache the *Americanos* want. White Hair gave me his word that he will try to take Delgadito alive."

"The word of a white-eye," Nantanh said in disgust. "Now there is something we can depend on." Most of the others smiled.

The old warrior's insult was like the thrust of a double-edged knife. It cut the whites, but it also cut Palacio for suggesting the Chiricahuas should do as the *Americanos* wanted. Palacio took the remark in stride, but he made a mental note to pay Nantanh back one day. He was not one to forgive an insult, no matter how slight.

"It seems we cannot reach agreement on this matter," Palacio said, "so maybe it is best if we spread the word among our people and let each warrior decide for himself whether he wants to aid White Hair or not."

"Anyone who does will never be welcome in my lodge," Nantanh said.

"I could never trust anyone who turned against one of our own," Chico said.

The meeting broke up, the leaders going their separate ways. Palacio had every reason to be disappointed by the end result, but he wasn't. He'd noticed that the youngest of those present, Giannah-tah, had not spoken in Delgadito's defense. Indeed, when the subject of the bounty came up, Palacio had seen a flicker of interest in the other's eyes.

Someone would take White Hair up on the offer, Palacio was sure. And when that happened, he stood to gain in three respects. First, the problem of what to do about White Apache would be solved once and for all. Second, he would finally be rid of Delgadito, who had been a thorn in his side for as long as he could remember. And third, he stood to gain in horses, blankets, and knives, because he had told the others that the whites-eyes were only offering half the number they actually were. The rest, naturally, would go to him.

Palacio grinned contentedly and motioned for one of his wives to bring him more *tizwin*. He deserved to celebrate a little. It wasn't every day that he deceived so many people at one time and ended up richer as a result. So what if some of those people were his very own? Stealing without being caught, that was the Apache way.

He couldn't help it if he was better at it than most.

On seeing the pair of cat-eyed Daniel Boones materialize out of the brush, Clay Taggart automatically lowered his right hand toward his Colt. He stopped when the one called Zeb, a lanky character whose lower lip had once been split by a knife or tomahawk, swung the muzzle of a big buffalo gun toward him and the hammer clicked back.

"I wouldn't, if I were you, Injun. This here Sharps will blow a hole in you the size of a pancake."

The tall man laughed. "Are you plumb loco, you jackass? Most of these rotten heathens don't speak our tongue, and even if this one does, odds are he wouldn't know a pancake if it was to bite him on the ass."

Marista walked up to her son and put an arm on Colletto's shoulders. "I speak white tongue," she boldly announced. "Who you be? What you want?"

Clay figured they were prospectors. Despite the risk and a ban by the Army on mining on the Chiricahua Reservation, scores of gold-hungry fools snuck onto Apache land every month. Most were caught and escorted off again. Some simply vanished.

Zeb ambled forward, his black whiskers creased by yellow teeth. "Imagine this! A squaw who savvies English. Why, next you know, Pike, they'll be wearin' frilly dresses and going to tea every afternoon."

Pike guffawed and advanced, leading a string

of horses, four of which were pack animals burdened with more supplies than a pair of prospectors rightfully needed, all covered over with canvas. "Ain't that a fact." He tied the lead animal to the cottonwood and turned. "As to who we are, squaw, and what we do, you might say that we're a travelin' tradin' post."

They were smugglers, Clay realized, hardcases who made their living selling ill-gotten goods on both sides of the border. Men without scruples, men who would as soon kill a man as look at him if there was profit to be made. More than ever he wanted to make a play for his Colt. But he wasn't about to commit suicide, and in his condition he wouldn't stand a prayer.

"You're a Pima, ain't you?" Zeb asked Marista. "You and the brat, both?"

"We are."

"And what about you?" Zeb said, moving closer to Clay and pressing the Sharps against his belly. "You sure as hell don't look like any Pima I ever saw."

"If I didn't know better, I'd swear he was an Apache," Pike said as he walked over behind Clay and claimed the Winchester and six-shooter.

"Can't be," Zeb said while scrutinizing Clay closely. "No self-respectin' Apache would let himself be caught flat-footed the way this one done." Pursing his lips, he paused. "There's something about this hombre, Pike."

"What?"

"I don't rightly know. But it sticks in my craw that I ought to know who he is. Reckon we've met him somewhere?"

Pike stood elbow to elbow with his companion. "The face ain't familiar, pard. But damn me if I don't think you're right." He slung Clay's rifle

69

over his own shoulder. "Now ain't this mighty strange."

Averting his gaze, Clay hoped they wouldn't notice the color of his eyes. It would be a dead giveaway of his identity, and once they knew who they had in their clutches, they were the types to gun him down where he stood and then tote his carcass to the fort to collect their blood money.

Zeb glanced at Clay's temple. "Looks as if he got himself shot not long ago. Nasty wound. Take a gander at all that pus oozin' out. I reckon he ain't long for this world if he don't get some doctorin'."

"So what do we do with them?"

The pair backed up a few feet. Pike gave the Pima woman the sort of look that left no doubt as to his intentions. Zeb scratched his bushy beard, pondering.

"Well, the woman should fetch a tidy sum from the Comanches. They'll take anything in a dress. As for the brat, we'll take him to Sonora and let the scalphunters have him, cheap. They'll be able to pass off his hair as genuine Apache."

"And this buck here?"

Zeb shrugged. "I can't rightly make up my mind. It makes sense to fill him full of lead, but I have this feelin' we should hold off a spell. And since we're not going anywhere until Palacio shows up, we might as well tie him up until we decide."

The mention of the Chiricahua chief perked Clay's interest. Now he knew why Palacio had been heading north. It made him wonder what sort of business the wily leader had with the two smugglers, but he didn't dwell on the question long.

Pike had gone to one of the pack animals

and was rummaging under the canvas. When he stepped back, he held a coiled rope. "Cover the buck for me, pard."

Clay tensed, his arms close to his sides. He wasn't about to let them hogtie him, hurt head or no. Once he was helpless, they were liable to beat him half to death for the hell of it. And there was no telling what they would do to the woman. They had taken his guns but not his knife, a mistake that would cost them when they came within reach.

Marista had steered Colletto closer to the stream. Her shoulders were slumped in meek surrender, her face bowed low. She had taken the water skin from her son and held it in front of her chest.

Zeb wagged the Sharps. "Don't give us no grief, Injun, or so help me, I'll blow one of your legs off at the knee." He switched to passable Chiricahua and repeated the warning, concluding with, "Do you understand me?"

By then Pike was near enough, a few steps to the rear of his partner. "Step aside and let me at him."

As Zeb started to comply, Clay exploded into action. Springing, he streaked the Bowie clear of its sheath and drove the gleaming blade at Zeb's gut. The smuggler, taken off guard, shifted and tried to train the Sharps on Clay's chest. The Bowie and the barrel clanged together. Whether by accident or by design, the rifle went off with a tremendous boom. The slug missed Clay by a finger's width, striking the cottonwood instead.

Zeb, throwing himself backward, collided with Pike.

Clay raised the knife to strike at the smuggler's neck, but before he could follow through, another bout of dizziness drew him up short. His limbs turned to mush.

"Move!" Pike roared, giving his partner a shove. "Let me finish this mangy varmint off here and now!"

Caught flat-footed, Clay could do no more than stand there helplessly as the smuggler took a deliberate bead on his forehead. He saw Pike's wicked grin of triumph, saw the smuggler's forefinger closing on the trigger.

Suddenly Pike threw back his head and screamed like a she-cat giving birth. The rifle fell from nerveless fingers as he stumbled a few feet, clawing at his back with both hands. He bent double, revealing the reason.

Marista had drawn a dagger from under her blouse and stabbed him squarely between the shoulder blades. Pike clutched at the hilt, but it was out of reach. As she wrenched it out, Zeb leaped to his friend's aid, clamped an arm around Pike's wrist, and scurried toward the vegetation.

Clay would have gone after them had his legs not turned traitor once more. He saw the Pima woman start to give chase, but she stopped when she glimpsed him fall. In the nick of time, she caught him. He planted both feet and rose, mumbling, "I'm fine. You can let go."

The brush had swallowed the smugglers. Clay could hear the crash and crackle of limbs receding rapidly. He was mildly surprised Zeb hadn't stood his ground and made a fight of it, but then, smugglers weren't famous for having a lot of courage; they were the human equivalent of rats and behaved accordingly.

Clay turned toward the horses, which had shied when the Sharps banged but had not run off. "We've got to light a shuck for other parts," he declared, "before they see fit to come back."

Marista gazed uncertainly at the animals. "You want us ride?"

"Yes." Clay could feel what little strength he had left ebbing swiftly. They had to leave before he collapsed, or they might never get out of there with there hides intact. Gripping her arm, he pulled her toward the string. "We have to skedaddle."

The Pima balked, a hint of fear in her face.

Mystified, Clay halted. "What the blazes is the matter?" he demanded, more gruffly than he meant to. It was outright ridiculous, her being afraid now when the whole day she had not shown the least bit of fright. He looked at the boy and discovered Colletto was equally rattled.

The horses were the answer. Clay recollected hearing somewhere that the Pimas and Maricopas had never mastered the horse, and even regarded the animals with a degree of superstitious awe. "Hell," he groused. "We don't have time for this nonsense."

Seizing Marista more firmly, Clay pulled her to the lead sorrel. Her eyes widened and she drew away. "You must," he said, slipping both arms around her waist. Bunching his shoulders, he spun, seeking to heave her onto the saddle. Before being shot he could have done so with ease. Now, he only swung her halfway up, and it took so much out of him that he nearly keeled over. In pure reflex, Marista grabbed hold of the saddle horn and held on.

Clay shoved her foot into the stirrup and pushed her the rest of the way. She appeared absolutely petrified and made no move to grip the reins, so he handed them to her. The boy offered no resistance as Clay hauled him over and placed him in front of the woman.

Pike had shoved Clay's Winchester into the boot on the second animal and placed Clay's Colt on the saddle. After picking up Pike's fallen rifle, Clay reclaimed both of his own guns, then forked leather and headed eastward along the stream. His head needed tending worse than ever but it would have to wait. He remembered that Zeb still had the single-shot Sharps, and he seemed to recall that Pike wore a revolver. At any moment the smugglers might open fire.

The trio fled at a gallop, the White Apache swaying, on the verge of collapse, the mother and son clinging to one another and their mount in abject terror.

Behind them, the brush parted and a gritty, wrathful face peered out "You vermin!" Zeb called out. "You haven't seen the last of us! Count on it!"

Chapter Six

Col. Reynolds was out of his bed and shaving when reveille sounded. The first note of the bugle brought a smile, for it meant the day was officially underway and he could get done all the things he wanted to do before taps and lights out.

For the first time in months Reynolds felt confident that he would soon deliver the White Apache's head to his superiors on a silver platter, as it were. Palacio had pledged the cooperation of the Chiricahuas, and in all their prior dealings the chief had always kept his word.

Reynolds hummed as he shaved. Putting an end to the white renegade would be quite a feather in his cap. It might even get him reassigned to a better post back East, maybe to a nice desk job in Washington. *Anywhere* else would be nice.

A scratching noise made the colonel glance down. A large scorpion was scuttling across the floor toward his naked feet, its upcurved tail raised to strike, its stinger moving back and forth as if seeking prey to puncture.

Col. Renolds let out a yelp and leaped backward. His legs connected with the wash basin and he tumbled in. Unfortunately, it contained no water, and he slammed his spine onto the rim. The pain was awful. Without thinking, he leaped back out again, and froze.

Something had crawled onto his right foot.

The colonel looked and swore he could feel the blood drain from his face. The grotesque tan creature was balanced on his instep, that dreadful stinger hovering close to his skin. He imitated a tree, his heart pounding wildly. His body broke out in a cold sweat from hairline to ankles.

The scorpion twisted, its pincers swinging from side to side.

Reynolds had seldom been so scared. He opened his mouth to call for help but decided not to. The shout might provoke the many legged horror into striking.

As if in answer to his prayers, there came a loud knock at the front door to his quarters. "Colonel? This is Sergeant McKinn. Are you all right in there? I thought I heard a crash."

The officer remembered telling the noncom to be at his quarters at six, and with his customary diligence, McKinn had arrived early. Forgetting himself, Reynolds went to answer, then choked off the words in his throat.

"Colonel? Are you here?" the sergeant hollered. "I'm coming in, sir."

Reynolds heard the door open and vowed to put the noncom up for promotion at the earliest opportunity. Footsteps came closer. A shadow moved across the floor of his bedroom, and a moment later the noncom's stocky form filled the doorway.

"Sir?" McKinn said, puzzled until he glanced down. "Sweet Jesus! Don't move." He snatched a towel from the rack and advanced slowly. "I'll try and knock it off you."

The scorpion raised its pincers higher and backed up against the commander's leg. Reynold's gulped, and shook his head. The sergeant was so intent on the scorpion that he didn't see. Again Reynolds tried, afraid the scorpion would accidentally sting him in self-defense.

McKinn noticed this time and stopped. "What do you want me to do, sir? Stand here and wait for it to crawl off?"

Mustering his courage, Col. Reynolds whispered, "Yes."

"I have a better idea, sir. Don't you worry."

Reynolds could hardly believe his eyes when the sergeant whirled and raced out. He listened for some clue as to the noncom's plan. A name was shouted, but he didn't hear it clearly. The seconds ticked by, each an eternity unto itself. His perspiration dried, making him so cold he had to resist an urge to shiver. The scorpion, meanwhile, had hunkered down as if content to stay there forever.

Just when Col. Reynolds was about ready to scream from impatience and frayed nerves, Sgt. McKinn returned—with one other. Into the bathroom glided Klo-sen, the Apache scout, the quiet Mescalero who had few equals at tracking. Without hesitation he walked on around behind Reynolds.

Sgt. McKinn stayed near the doorway. "It'll just be a few moments now, sir. He's an old hand at this."

At what? Reynolds wondered. And almost jumped out of his skin when a copper hand holding a long knife appeared beside his right leg, next to his knee. He watched in riveted fascination as the slender blade slowly descended. A moment of panic seized him as he imagined the savage stabbing the scorpion while it sat on his foot.

"He's about ready, sir," McKinn said.

The knife dipped so low that it nearly scraped the scorpion's tail. The scorpion was facing the doorway and hadn't moved in quite some time.

Klo-sen leaned forward so that his head was next to the commander's leg. With delicate skill he eased the blade between Reynolds's ankle and the scorpion. Then, with a deft flip, he sent the scorpion sailing.

Sgt. McKinn was ready. As the scorpion slid across the floor toward him, he raised his boot on high and stamped. The crunch was loud in the confined bathroom. "There you go, sir," he said, lifting his boot to show the mangled mass underneath.

Col. Reynolds had to swallow a few times before he could respond. "You have my gratitude, Sergeant. You and Klo-sen."

The Apache had sheathed his knife. He walked to the door, then glanced back. "Maybe you see more, White Hair," he said in clipped English.

"I beg your pardon?" Reynolds said.

Klo-sen pointed at the mess on the floor. "Female. Make home here. Maybe many little ones around." Nodding curtly, he departed.

"Wonderful," Col. Reynolds said to himself.

"Anything else I can do for you, sir?" Sgt. McKinn asked.

"Not at the moment." The noncom saluted and left.

Reynolds quickly finished shaving, glancing at the floor every few seconds. After donning his uniform, he doublechecked his boots by upending them and slapping the soles, slid them on, and hustled out into the already warm sunshine. The troops were in formation, about to be put through their morning drill by McKinn.

The commander crossed to the officer's mess and was pleased to find all the junior officers in attendance, as he had requested. Taking his seat at the head of the table, he swept them all with a probing stare and said, "Good morning, gentlemen. By now I expect that all of you have heard the latest scuttlebutt. For those of you who might be skeptical, it's true. I've solicited the aid of the chief of the Chiricahuas in an effort to bring the White Apache and Delgadito to bay."

"Can you trust Palacio, sir?" Capt. Forester interrupted.

"I wouldn't trust that fat barbarian to water my horse," Reynolds said. "But he's not helping us because he's a pillar of red society. He's motivated by greed, pure and simple." Reynolds waited to see if anyone else would question his judgment but none had the veteran's temerity. "I don't know when Palacio will contact us. It might be today, it might be two weeks from now. But whenever it is, I intend to be ready to respond at a moment's notice."

Lt. James Peterson, the junior officer at the post, raised his hand. He was fresh out of the Academy, where he had had the dubious distinction of being ranked last in his graduating class. "Sir, I'd like to volunteer to lead the patrol that goes after this White Apache character when the times comes. Give me twenty-five good men and we can whip the renegades without working up a sweat."

Several of the older officers smiled. Capt. Forester glanced at the lieutenant, then rolled his eyes at the ceiling.

Col. Reynolds sighed. Far too many green officers had lost their lives on the frontier simply because they were too headstrong for their own good and as ignorant as a rock. "I appreciate your enthusiasm," he said tactfully, "but I've already picked the officer who will go after Taggart. In a situation like this, with the lives of so many innocents at stake if the renegades aren't stopped, I have to go with the most experienced man I have, and that would be Capt. Forester."

The lieutenant frowned but held his peace.

"Forester," Reynolds went on, "I want you to get together with Sgt. McKinn. Handpick the forty best soldiers at the fort. Organize them into a separate unit, answerable only to me. My Flying Detachment, as I like to call it."

"Yes, sir."

"The men you choose will be relieved from all normal duties until further notice. I want them fully equipped and whipped into shape within four days."

"Only four, sir?"

"You heard me. When Palacio contacts us, I want the Flying Detachment ready to fly to wherever the renegades are supposed to be holed up. By cutting down our response time, we increase the odds of success."

Forester nodded. "Consider it done."

Col. Reynolds glanced at Capt. Vincent Parmalee, who was close to dozing off. "One more thing," he added. "The Flying Detachment won't be going into battle alone. All seven Apache scouts and the officer in charge of them are to assist you. He will, of course, be under your direct command while in the field."

The orders jolted Capt. Parmalee half out of his seat. "Me, sir?" he bleated.

"You *are* the Chief of Scouts," Reynolds said.

"I know, sir," Parmalee said. He squirmed and licked his lips. "But I rarely go out with them. The Apaches work better under a minimum of supervision—"

"Spare me, Captain," Reynolds snapped. "So far the scouts have proven useless at finding the renegades. Maybe they'll perform better when you're out there with them to spur them on."

"But sir—"

The commander gestured for silence. "I'll brook no argument, Parmalee. You're going along, and that's final." He paused. "Look at the bright side. It might do you some good."

"Sir?" the captain said bleakly.

"You've been looking a little peaked of late. That's what comes of always being indoors and never getting enough exercise. Getting out in the sun and fresh air will do wonders for your constitution."

"If you say so, sir."

"I do." Reynolds was about to instruct the cook to serve breakfast when he thought of one final item. "Oh. Capt. Parmalee. From this day on, Klo-sen is to be the Assistant Chief of Scouts. He is being promoted to the rank of corporal. You will attend to the necessary paperwork and inform him at your earliest convenience."

Parmalee flushed crimson. "Sir, with all due respect, I don't need an assistant. It will undermine my authority."

"The Apaches might think differently. I believe

they'll welcome having one of their own act as go-between," Col. Reynolds said, and clapped his hands to signal the discussion at an end. "Now let's eat, shall we, men?" He smiled broadly. "I don't know about the rest of you, but I have the feeling our luck has finally turned and the White Apache is as good as ours."

Clay Taggart became aware of a damp, cool sensation on his brow. He stayed still with his eyes closed, trying to recollect what had happened to him. He remembered the shooting scrape with the smugglers, remembered fleeing eastward at a gallop for several miles and then feeling so dizzy and weak that he had been unable to stay in the saddle.

A soft hand touched his cheek. Close by, flames crackled. Water gurgled, indicating the stream was not far off. Clay opened his eyes.

A small fire had been built in a grassy glade almost at the water's edge. Colletto was busy skinning a rabbit, using his mother's dagger. Marista was on her knees beside him, a pan filled with water at her side. She removed a folded white cloth from his forehead, dipped it in the pan, and wrung out the excess. As she did so, she noticed he was awake. "At last," she said. "How you feel?"

"Better," Clay said. And it was true. The pounding in his head was mostly gone, and other than a dull ache where the bullet had glanced off his temple, there was no pain. "How long have I been out?"

The Pima woman jabbed her thumb skyward, where a myriad of stars twinkled like fireflies. "Two sleeps."

"That long?" Clay started to sit up but she placed a hand on his chest.

Blood Treachery

"You rest. Eat. Drink. Still very weak."

She had a point, Clay mused. He did feel woozy. His blood seemed to be pumping at a snail's pace, while his arms felt as heavy as two buffaloes. "What about Zeb and Pike? Has there been any sign of the smugglers?"

"No."

Clay let himself relax. Apparently the pair had elected not to follow, or they would have caught up by now. After he recovered, he would go find Delgadito and the others and persuade the Apaches to help track the smugglers down. The sons of bitches were going to pay, once they answered a few questions about their connection to Palacio.

"Son make stew," Marista informed him. "You maybe hungry now?"

"Are you kidding? I could swallow a horse, whole," Clay told her.

She gently placed the moist cloth over his brow again. "This and pan take off horse. Hope you not mind."

"Why would I?"

"Yours now, yes?"

Clay gazed at the string tethered across the clearing. Since he had seen fit to make off with the animals, the horses and everything on them were his plunder. "I don't mind at all," he responded, then mentioned without thinking, "What's mine is yours. Use whatever you need."

Marista visibly tensed. "Why you so kind?"

"Why shouldn't I be?" Clay retorted. "You've saved my life several times over. The least I can do is repay your kindness as best I can."

She stared at him a bit, then moved off to help prepare a stew, leaving Clay to his thoughts. He bent his neck to find the Colt in its holster and the Winchester at his elbow. It was a good sign; she trusted him enough not to have taken his weapons. Twisting, he saw the saddles and supplies piled neatly a dozen feet away. Given the Pima fear of horses, it showed great courage on her part to have stripped them down. He told her as much when she came over bearing a cup of hot broth.

"Had to do," Marista said.

Clay held the cup and talked her into dragging a saddle over for him to lean on. He sipped slowly. It had been so long since he had eaten last that the broth seared his throat like molten lava. His stomach did flip-flops for a while, but eventually he polished off the cup and was ready for more.

Marista hesitated before rising. "Must ask question," she said, rather timidly but forcefully. "Sorry, but must."

"Ask anything you want," Clay said. She shared a glance with the boy, whose worried look led Clay to suspect what was coming.

Plainly nervous, Marista said, "Your hair like Apache. Your clothes like Apache. Your skin dark like Apache. But you be white man."

Clay waited.

"We hear stories. Hear of white man turn on own people. Ride with Apaches, kill like Apaches. Kill whites, kill Mexicans, kill everyone. White Apache, he be called." Marista's gaze bored into him. "That be you, Clay Taggart?"

There was no sense in denying the truth, so Clay nodded. "I'm your huckleberry. But don't let it upset you none. I wouldn't harm a hair on your pretty head, yours or the boy's. I hope you'll take me at my word when I tell you that I'm not the cold-blooded fiend they make me out to be."

Clay wished he was able to read her mind so he'd know how she was reacting to the news. He couldn't blame her if she were to up and leave, and he certainly wouldn't try to stop her. But he didn't want her to go. He'd grown fond of her company. Quite fond. So he was all the more elated when she said the one thing that showed maybe, just maybe, his interest in her was returned.

"You think my head pretty?"

"One of the prettiest," Clay declared. "Fact is, I wouldn't be at all surprised if a fine filly such as yourself has a husband stashed away somewhere. Although why he'd let you wander Apache country by yourself is beyond me."

A cloud darkened Marista's features and she looked into the night. Hoping to prod the truth from her, Clay added, "If you want, I'll be more than happy to escort the two of you back to your village after I mend."

"Never go back. Ever."

"What? Why?" Clay inquired, at a loss to comprehend. The Pimas were a close-knit people who stuck together through thick and thin. She was bound to have kin somewhere willing to put the boy and her up for a spell.

"Can not go back," Marista emphasized bitterly.

"But what about your husband? Where is he? Is he alive?" Clay probed. She had to have had a husband at one time. The idea of a Pima woman having a child out of wedlock was unthinkable, since the Pimas were as noted for their chastity as the Apaches.

The woman let out a long breath, her shoulders drooping. "Husband not want," she said, scarcely above a whisper.

"Not want?" Clay said, unsure whether he had

85

heard correctly. "Is the man plumb loco? How can he not want a beautiful woman like you?"

"My husband Culozul."

The way she said it, Clay got the idea she thought it would explain everything. But the revelation only confused him more. Culozul was the name of a prominent Pima chief who had been written up in the Tucson newspaper a while back when he visited Washington D.C. The paper had gone on and on about how impressed the chief had been by all he saw, stressing again and again how superior the white culture was to the red.

The reporter had done his best to portray the chief in a comical light, telling how he gawked at street lights and steam engines and such, and how Culozul always scratched himself in public.

Clay had read the article. He remembered laughing when it was revealed that the chief had scandalized himself at a formal banquet by tearing into the food with his hands and teeth instead of using silverware. But back in those days he had laughed at anything that poked fun at Indians.

In a twisted manner, Culozul was famous. Now here was this beautiful woman claiming to be his wife. Clay scratched his head and said, "I've heard of him. Seems to me you must be wrong. He'll be right pleased to get you back safe and sound."

Marista bunched her fist and made a motion as if flinging an object to the ground. "Him cast me out. Never see again or I be killed."

Clay figured she was spinning a yarn. The Pimas would never tolerate murder. It was against tribal custom. There was only one exception that he knew of: they allowed women caught in the act of adultery to be stoned to death. Or shunned as outcasts. At the thought, he stiffened. "Culozul caught you with another man and had you kicked out of the village?"

The woman turned on him, anger and pain fighting for dominance. "I never sleep other man!" she said passionately. "Never do!" Her eyes moistened and she blinked, fighting back tears of frustration. "Culozul say I do. Not true. Him lie."

Clay knew he had already pried more deeply than he had any right to do, but he couldn't help himself. "Why would he do a thing like that?"

Her answer crackled with loathing. "Him want other woman. Younger woman."

Clay glanced at the boy, whose expression was cast in granite. "Your son ran off with you when you were thrown out?" he hazarded a guess.

"Colletto hates Culozul. Him want kill his father."

Enough had been disclosed. Clay asked no more questions. He stared into the fire, thinking of the terrible ordeal the woman had gone through, an ordeal in some respects similar to his own. Like him, she had been betrayed by the one she loved the most. Like him, she had been unjustly accused. Like him, she had been made an outcast.

More than ever, Clay admired her grit. She had headed off into the wilderness to fend for herself and the boy, never knowing from one day to the next how she would make ends meet or whether she would be alive to greet the next dawn. Damned if she didn't remind him of himself.

"You want we go now?"

The query startled Clay. "What gives you that idea? Hell, no, I don't want you to leave," he stated. "Fact is, I'm grateful for the company. If you want, you're welcome to tag along with me a spell. But I've got to warn you up front. Staying with me might not be too smart. I've got a price on my head. Every time I turn around, someone is trying to plant me six feet under."

As if to accent the point, in the darkness behind them a gun hammer clicked and the familiar voice of Zeb declared, "Do tell. Raise those hands of yours high, White Apache, or you die where you sit."

Chapter Seven

Delgadito had always liked the wind. It cooled him on hot days, brought news of rain long before clouds gathered, and carried the scent of enemies and game to his sensitive nostrils to alert him. The wind was his friend.

This night, late, his friend carried to his keen ears the faint rattle of a pebble. Instantly Delgadito was up and in a crouch, his rifle clutched at his waist. "Someone comes," he whispered.

Fiero was off the ground in a flash, shaking his head to dispel lingering tendrils of sleep. It bothered him that the other warrior's senses had proven more acute. He took immense pride in the fact many Chiricahuas considered him one of the best warriors in the tribe, and he did not like to be shown up. Fiero lived only to fight, to excel at war, to kill white-eyes and *Nakai-yes* until the rest were driven from Apache land.

The shelf on which the pair had made camp was situated high on a ridge overlooking a barren canyon. On one side lay a steep drop, hundreds of feet, while on the other was a gravel slope no living creature could climb without making noise.

The wind brought them no new sounds, so Delgadito crept to the rim and peered down the slope. At the limits of his vision a form moved, gliding toward them. He motioned at Fiero, who cat-footed off to the left and eased onto his stomach.

Delgadito did likewise. He had a fair idea who was down there but he was not about to take anything for granted. He moved to a point that afforded a clear view of the gravel strip and tucked his rifle to his shoulder.

Only a short while passed before the night air rang to the high-pitched bark-bark-bark of an agitated chipmunk, just such a sound as a chipmunk might make if disturbed in its burrow by a roving predator.

From Delgadito's lips issued an answer, as perfect as the original, so much so that a real chipmunk would have been fooled. A shape glided from the boulders and up the incline. Delgadito looked but saw no others and right away he knew that something was wrong. "You come alone, Ponce," he said as he stood.

The young warrior had been running for hours. He was tired and thirsty and his legs were sore but he was not about to let the two older men know. "Cuchillo Negro sent me on ahead," he reported.

Fiero loomed out of the night. "Why? What has happened?"

"*Lickoyee-shis-inday* never joined us as he was

supposed to. Cuchillo Negro went in search of him and sent me ahead to let you know."

"I told White Apache not to go," Delgadito said harshly. "Leaving heads for the white-eyes to find is foolish. It serves no real purpose."

"I like the idea," Fiero declared. "It shows the white-eyes that we are not afraid, that they will pay for taking our land and making our people live like dogs."

"All it does is stir them up to come look for us," Delgadito said. "I would rather they cower in their stone lodges so we can do as we please without interference."

Ponce had heard the merits debated many times and he made bold to comment, "White Apache says it strikes fear into their hearts. And who should know better than him since he was a white-eye before he became one of us?"

Delgadito had to clamp his mouth shut to keep from making a remark he might regret. He was the one who had given Clay Taggart the Apache name of *Lickoyee-shis-inday*, but he had not meant for anyone to take him seriously. It had been shortly after he saved the white-eye from the lynch party, when Taggart had been a stumbling simpleton who couldn't last three days in the wild without help.

How could anyone have foreseen what would occur? Delgadito reflected. Taggart, saving his life. Taggart, learning Chiricahua ways so readily it amazed even Delgadito. Taggart, becoming a respected member of the band, the man whose counsel the others sought when important decisions were to be made. Taggart, who had replaced Delgadito as leader. It was enough to make him want to scream with fury.

But whenever Delgadito felt his resentment

build, he reminded himself that White Apache had saved his life several times over, that if not for Clay Taggart his war against the whites would have ended in disaster many moons ago.

Delgadito had to possess himself with patience. Thanks to White Apache, the band had raided far and wide with sterling success, and tales of their prowess were a common topic around campfires at the reservation. Soon, now, the band would grow in size as young warriors flocked to join them. And when the band was big enough to suit him, he would find a means of taking up the reins of leadership once more. All he needed was patience.

"We waste time standing here," Fiero said. "I am ready to go this moment."

"And I," Ponce said, although he would rather sleep the rest of the night through.

"Then we will go," Delgadito said.

Like three tawny panthers they bounded over the rim and were soon shrouded in darkness.

Lightning reflexes sometimes work of their own accord. So although Clay Taggart heard a gun cocked and the smuggler warn him not to move, he autmically reached for his Colt and started to whirl.

A hard object jolted against the back of Clay's head. He went rigid, unwilling to risk being bashed on the noggin just when he was beginning to recover from his wound.

"I'd make wolf meat of you this minute, Taggart, but I'm not about to lug your smelly carcass all the way to the nearest fort to collect the reward," Zeb said, stepping around to where he could cover the three of them with that big Sharps of his. "The heat tends to ripen a corpse real quick hereabouts."

"So you know who I am," Clay said, intending to keep the man distracted while he racked his brain for a means of turning the tables.

"It hit me while I was mendin' my pard," Zeb said. "Those blue eyes of yours are a dead giveaway." He snickered. "Then I heard you spillin' your guts to the squaw here and knew for sure I'd hit the mother lode."

"Where's your friend?"

"He's hurtin' real bad so I left him lyin' out in the brush a piece." Zeb pivoted and hollered at the top of his lungs. "Pike! Haul your ass in here. I've got 'em!"

Clay was desperate to do something. But what? If he made a grab for a weapon, he'd be shot before he could bring it into play. The Pimas would be no help. Marista had frozen, her hands on her knees. The boy appeared flabbergasted, hunkered there with the rabbit hide draped over one leg.

Zeb took another step. "Did you really think we wouldn't come after you, renegade? It took us a while, what with Pike feelin' so poorly, but we weren't about to let you make off with all our goods. I'm surprised you didn't keep on a goin'."

"We didn't have much choice," Clay said lamely. In the distance a twig snapped. It wouldn't be long before they had him disarmed and hogtied. He was a goner unless he made a move. But the smuggler was watching him like the proverbial hawk.

"Pike has been lookin' forward to seein' the three of you again, bastard," Zeb said. "Especially the squaw. Her dagger done put a nasty hole in him. Put an ear to it, and you can hear his lungs workin'."

To the surprise of both men, Marista spoke. "Him hurt bad? Very sorry."

"You are?" Zeb replied.

"Sorry not kill him," the woman said sweetly, and grinned, a mocking, taunting grin calculated to rile any man.

It riled the smuggler. Cursing lustily, Zeb moved toward her and raised the Sharps to smash her with the stock. He was so mad that all he could think of was wiping that smirk off her face. Her face was all he concentrated on, when he should have been watching elsewhere.

Clay saw Marista's hands drop to the pan and divined her purpose even as her fingers closed on the rim.

Zeb was almost upon her when she swept her arms upward and heaved the water full in his face. The smuggler recoiled and lowered the Sharps, his curses a strident litany of hate. For a second or two his vision was blurred, and he blinked to clear it.

Those two seconds were all Clay Taggart needed. Like most Arizona ranchers, he was uncommonly handy with a six-shooter, thanks in part to his pa, who had taught him to shoot as soon as he was old enough to hold a pistol. For years a six-gun had been one of the many tools he had used on his ranch, a tool little different from his hammer or hoe in that it had a specific use, namely to kill rattlers and protect him from marauding war parties.

Clay had practiced often. On several occasions he had entered the annual Tucson marksmanship contest and finished in the top five. He could unlimber his hardware so fast his hand was a blur and empty the cylinder in less time than it took to tell about it.

Blood Treachery

To a seasoned gun hand, two seconds was an eternity.

Clay cleared leather as the water struck Zeb. His draw was a shade slow because he was seated and at an awkward angle, but it was still plenty quick, so quick that he banged off two swift shots before Zeb realized he had drawn.

The smuggler twisted to level the Sharps, but the impact of the slugs punched him backward and jerked him half around. The rifle fell from arms suddenly grown limp. He looked down at it, then at the twin holes oozing blood in his chest. "Well, I'll be damned!" he said weakly. His legs gave way and he fell to his knees.

Clay, with an effort, rose to his own. The shots would forewarn Pike, who might try to pick them off. They had to get away from the fire, from the light. Suddenly Marista was at his side, assisting him, and he managed to stand.

Zeb was still alive, his arms convulsing, his mouth twitching. He glared at them, at Clay, and spat, "Finish it!"

Obliging, Clay cored the man's brain. Then, with the boy following, he hurried into the darkness. He felt stronger than he had in days but still not quite strong enough to get very far on his own, and he was grateful for Marista's help.

Colletto abruptly called out and pointed.

The other smuggler materialized out of the night, walking stiffly toward them, his legs thudding the ground heavily as if each step was a monumental exertion.

Clay halted, shifted, and was all set to shoot when he noticed that Pike's hands were empty. The man had the most peculiar expression, a blank sort of look with his eyes as wide as walnuts and his mouth gaping open. Clay tensed, wary of a trick, but Pike made no sudden moves. A few seconds later he found out why.

Pike crumpled as if all his bones had changed to mush. Slowly spinning to the earth, he thudded onto his stomach, revealing the black hilt of a long knife that jutted from between his shoulder blades.

"How—?" Marista said, and gasped.

From out of nowhere another man appeared, a full-blooded Apache who carried a rifle in the crook of an elbow and stood impassively next to the body. In a fluid move, he tore the knife out, wiped the blade clean on the dead smuggler's buckskin shirt, and straightened. "*Tu no vale nada*," he addressed the corpse. Then, advancing, he raised a hand in salute and said in greeting, "*Lickoyee-shis-inday, nejeunee.*"

"*Nejeunee*, Cuchillo Negro," White Apache responded, overjoyed to see his friend again. "My brother comes at just the right time."

"I have been searching for you long and hard," the warrior declared, stopping to stare at Zeb. "It makes my heart glad to see you are well."

"The others?"

"*Shee-dah.* Ponce went after them. They should be here before the moon rises again."

White Apache gestured. "Sit. Rest. Share our stew." He introduced the Pima woman and her boy, who had shied close together and were regarding Black Knife as they might their executioner.

"Is she yours?" Cuchillo Negro asked in the Chiricahua tongue.

Clay glanced at her. If he said no, the warrior might elect to take her for himself, which by Apache custom he had every right to do. There would be nothing Clay could do about it. But if he said yes, he was making a false claim, lying, in effect, to one of the few friends he had in the world. Switching to English, he told Marista, "He wants to know if you're my woman. Do you know what that means?"

Without missing a beat, she said, "Tell him I be your woman."

"I'd rather not lie," Clay said. "If you want to go your own way with the boy, feel free. I'll persuade my friend to let you be. I'll tell him I owe you a debt."

Marista faced him and threw her shoulders back. "I be your woman. If you want us."

Her emphasis on the last word wasn't lost on Clay. "Do you know what you're letting yourself in for? It won't be easy. None of us might live out the year."

She came over and gently placed a hand on his cheek. "You be kind man, Clay Taggart. I see it in eyes, feel it my heart. You strong man. Good man."

"Hell, I've been called a lot of things lately, but not that." Clay grinned wryly. "Most every soul in the Territory wants to see me strung up or staked out as buzzard bait."

Marista nodded at the wilderness encircling them. "Hard land. Hard for us live. Savvy, Clay Taggart? We have no one. You have no one. We belong with you."

Her simple eloquence brought a lump to Clay's throat. He hardly knew her, yet he cared for her a great deal, more than he had ever cared for any woman except Lilly. They shared a bond that came from deep within them. It was unexpected, it was strange, it was glorious. Before he realized what he was doing, he had bent and kissed her lightly on the mouth.

Marista smiled and touched her lips. Colletto gasped. Cuchillo Negro grinned and said, "I have my answer, White Apache. And I hope, my brother, that you know what you are doing."

"You are not the only one," Clay said, troubled by thoughts of the horrible fate that might befall the Pimas if they stuck with him. He didn't want to be responsible for their deaths, indirectly or otherwise. There had to be a place they could go to lie low where the woman and her son would be safe, or as safe as it was possible to be with every white in Arizona gunning for him.

Clay brought up the subject later, after polishing off three delicious helpings of stew. The food did wonders for his well being. He felt strong again, almost whole, almost his old self.

Cuchillo Negro listened attentively and replied, "I know Chiricahua country as well as any man. There is one place I can think of where your woman will not be found. It is called Eagle's Roost."

"Tell me about it," Clay urged eagerly.

"It is a cave deep in the mountains where few ever go, even Chiricahuas. The land is steep and there are many ravines. The only approach is up a winding trail. Horses cannot get close."

"Why do the Chiricahuas not go there? Is there no water? Is the hunting poor?"

"There is a spring in the cave. Game is scarce, but the real reason is that many believe Eagle's Roost is bad medicine. They think it is home to an evil mountain spirit."

Clay grunted. Since joining the renegades he had learned more than any white man alive about Apache beliefs and practices. He knew they believed in a supreme deity they called *Yusn*—the Giver of Life. They also believed in a host of lesser spirits, among them the powerful *Gans*, or mountain spirits.

The Apaches, by white standards, were highly superstitious. They feared witches, dreaded touching the dead, and were highly secretive about their burial customs. When an Apache died from disease, his wickiup and all his possessions were burned, and the spot was shunned forever after.

It was accepted by them that their everyday lives were under the direct influence of many evil spirits that had to be appeased or catastrophe would result. As a result, the Apaches had many rituals to ward off evil powers, illness and the like.

Eagle's Roost sounded like just the kind of hideout Clay needed, but there was one hitch. "What about you and the other warriors?" he asked. "Will all of you go to the cave with me?"

"I cannot speak for Delgadito and the rest, only for myself," Cuchillo Negro said. "While I do not like to tempt the Gans, I also do not want my white brother to think I am afraid. If you go, White Apache, I will go. But I warn you, brother to brother, not to. It is not wise to tempt the *Gans*. Something very bad will happen."

The earnest appeal almost, but not quite, convinced Clay. But he wasn't about to be scared off by a silly superstition. If Eagle's Roost was the safest place for the woman and boy to be, then that was where they would go.

Two hours shy of sundown the next day, Delgadito, Fiero, and Ponce arrived. They had pushed themselves, and it showed in their fatigued features.

Delgadito had insisted on the grueling pace. As

much as he despised White Apache, he was not about to let anything happen to the one man who could help him regain the position of leadership he coveted more than life itself. He would do all in his power to keep the white-eye alive—until he was chief again.

Clay was elated to see them. At last, events were going his way. The band was reunited. The swelling had gone completely away and the wound was mending nicely. He was fit to travel. And he now had a woman to call his own.

On seeing the trio approach the camp, Clay jumped to his feet and ran to greet them. In his excitement he clapped Delgadito on the shoulder and said happily, "Glad to see you again, pard. For a while there it was nip and tuck, and I didn't know if I'd ever be able to pay you back for all you've done for me."

"You will," Delgadito said in his thickly accented English. For months now he had been diligently trying to learn the white tongue, but try as he might he couldn't shed the accent.

They had made a deal, the two of them. Delgadito had agreed to teach Clay the Chiricahua tongue if Clay taught him English. Of the pair, Clay proved to be the better pupil, much to Delgadito's chagrin.

The newcomers were surprised to find the Pimas there. Fiero listened to Clay's explanation, then growled, "You make a mistake, *Lickoyee-shis-inday*. I know all of you think we need women to make our band whole again. But these two will slow us down, make us easy prey for the blue coats."

"You make the mistake," Clay shot back, since to give an inch to Fiero made him take a yard. "They will not slow us down because they will not be with us. I am taking them to Eagle's Roost to stay."

It was as if a celestial puppeteer had yanked on the strings of three Chiricahua puppets. The heads of all three jerked up, and Delgadito said, "Eagle's Roost is bad medicine. Cuchillo Negro should have told you."

"He did," Clay said, "but I am going anyway, and he is going with me."

Delgadito glanced at Black Knife. "Has the sun roasted your brain? The mountain spirit will punish whoever dares step foot in that cave. Did you tell him the story?"

"What story?" Clay asked.

Cuchillo Negro had sat calmly sharpening his knife the whole time. Now he set the whetstone in his lap and said, "There is a reason Eagle's Roost is shunned by our people." He tested the blade on his thumb and smiled when it drew blood. "Many winters ago it was customary for many to use the cave since it is the only source of water for several sleeps around. Hunting parties passing through the area, raiders heading north to attack the whites, they would all spend a night or two there. Sometimes a warrior would take his family just to be alone with them for a few days."

"An Apache hotel," Clay quipped in English, but Delgadito failed to see the humor.

"One day a warrior named Toga-de-chuz and his woman went to Eagle's Roost. It was customary for whoever stayed in the cave to burn an offering when they first entered to appease the mountain spirit who lives there. But Toga-de-chuz spurned the *Gans*. He did not make an offering, and late that night his wife woke up to his screams and saw him being stabbed by his own knife."

Clay digested the tale, then said, "Stabbed how? By his own hand?"

"No. No one held the hilt. It floated in the air, stabbing again and again."

"How do you know this?"

"The woman saw it all. She was too terrified to help her man, and when he was dead, she cowered under her blanket until daylight, then fled. Since then Eagle's Roost has been bad medicine."

Skeptical, to say the least, Clay held his tongue. He would only offend his friends if he told them that he suspected the woman had killed her husband and blamed it on a nonexistent spirit. She had been shrewd in that regard. For a wife to kill her husband merited death.

"So what do you say, White Apache?" Delgadito asked in English. "Do you still intend to take the Pima there?"

"I do," Clay confirmed. "And I would be obliged if all of you would tag along. We can hide out there for a spell and plan our next raid."

Delgadito had half a mind to refuse. But he was committed to a course of action that required him to stay with the white-eye, like it or not, so he said, "We will come. But heed my words. The mountain spirit will be angry with us."

Clay Taggart smiled. He could live with that, he told himself.

Little did he know.

Chapter Eight

It was Dandy Jim who spotted the buzzards and pointed them out to Capt. Henry Derrick. The officer immediately halted the patrol and pulled out his field glasses.

Derrick had served in the Arizona Territory for slightly over a year. He was a competent, tough campaigner and a close personal friend of Capt. Gerald Forester. It was Forester who had taken Derrick under his wing when Derrick arrived at Fort Bowie and taught him all he needed to know to survive the relentless war against the Apaches.

One of the first rules of combat, as Forester had put it, was, "Jackasses rush in where cooler heads know to tread softly. Always check out the lay of the land before committing yourself and your men. Apaches love to lie in ambush."

Now Derrick did just that, studying the seven buzzards he could see wheeling high in the sky and the chaparral beneath them. He wouldn't put it past the renegades to kill some animal and leave it there so circling buzzards would lure the curious to their doom. Or perhaps the Apaches had spotted his patrol from a distance and set the trap up. Whatever the case, Derrick was not about to let himself be outfoxed. Turning to his two scouts, Dandy Jim and Dead Shot, both Cibicu Indians, he pointed and commanded, "Check it out and report back to me on the double."

Dandy Jim, who liked to wear an old frock coat, of all things, and a big white feather in his blue headband, said, "We go see plenty quick."

As the scouts galloped off, Derrick ordered Sgt. Bryce to have the troopers see to their carbines and pistols. If there was to be an engagement, the renegades would pay dearly. He kept his field glasses trained on the brush until Dead Shot appeared and waved.

At a trot Captain Derrick led the patrol to trees bordering a stream he had not even known was there. In a glade near the water they came on the bodies of two white men.

Both had been stripped naked but not mutilated. The buzzards had been at them, though, and their eyeballs had been gouged out, their noses pecked clean off, and their tongues ripped from their mouths.

"I recognize that small one, sir," Sergeant Bryce said. "His name is Zeb Plunkett. He's been in trouble with the law a few times. For the past ten years or so he's made his living as a smuggler, working the border country."

"Well, his smuggling days are over," Derrick commented. "Select a burial detail and see they are laid to rest."

"Yes, sir."

Blood Treachery

The two Cibicues had been prowling the area, eyes glued to the ground. After a while they hurried over and Dandy Jim, who knew more English, reported.

"Find tracks. Apaches do this." A gleam came into the scout's dark eyes. "One white man with them. He wear Apache moccasins."

Captain Derrick felt his pulse race. "How do you know it's a white man?"

Dandy Jim extended his right leg and held his foot so the toes pointed inward. "Indian walk like this." Pivoting, he pointed the toes outward. "White man always walk like this."

"Could it be the White Apache?"

"Maybe so," Dandy Jim said.

"Then we'll go after them as soon as the smugglers are planted," Derrick said, barely able to credit his good fortune. Every officer in Arizona was on the lookout for the notorious traitor; whoever brought Clay Taggart in would have his career made, as it were.

"One more thing," Dandy Jim said. "They have woman, boy with them."

"You don't say?"

"Pimas. Can tell by moccasins they wear."

The officer knew enough about the various tribes to remark, "Pimas running with Apaches? It was my understanding that they're mortal enemies."

"Sometimes Apaches steal Pima women," the Cibicu said, and leered suggestively.

Derrick had not heard of any recent Apache raids on Pima villages, but he tabled his doubts for the time being. *If* the scout was right, and *if* this was the White Apache's band, and *if* they did have a woman and boy along, it presented a golden opportunity which he was not about to pass up. "How far ahead of us are they?"

"Band leave here at first light. White Apache ride. Woman, boy on same animal. Rest on foot, leading other horses."

Twisting, the captain noted the position of the sun. Another lesson Forester had imparted was how to tell time by the sun and stars. Watches were prone to malfunction in the field, the veteran had pointed out.

Derrick judged the time to be close to ten o'clock. Out of habit he verified it by consulting his pocket watch. "That gives them no more than a four hour head start. If they're moving slowly, we can overtake them by nightfall."

The officer swung toward the burial detail. "Get a move on, Sergeant," he barked. "They're just a pair of smugglers, for crying out loud. Sprinkle some dirt on them, cover them with rocks, and be done with it."

In under five minutes the troopers were all mounted. At Derrick's signal, the patrol moved out, going at a brisk walk, the scouts well in the lead.

This was new country to Derrick. He had ranged over a good portion of the vast Chiricahua Reservation but seldom into the interior, into the heart of the mountain fastness where the renegades were rumored to have their strongholds.

It seemed only logical to Derrick and Forester and other seasoned officers to strike at the renegades where they were least likely to expect attack, but the higher-ups at headquarters had given explicit orders to the effect that no patrols were to penetrate into the heart of the reservation unless under specific directions to do so. Derrick, however, was not above disobeying the command in order to get his hands on the White Apache. If need be, he would dog the renegade to the gates of Hell. Headquarters would overlook the indiscretion if he brought in Taggart's bullet-ridden corpse.

For the next several hours Capt. Derrick pushed the horses hard, resting them five minutes out of every sixty. He had ample time to reflect on the man he was after, and to recall what little information he knew about his quarry.

Clay Taggart had been caught in the act of raping a neighbor's wife, had shot the cowpuncher who stumbled on them, then had fled deep into the Chiricahua Mountains. Everyone had about given him up for dead when reports filtered in of a band of Apaches being led by a white man. At first the Army had scoffed. But as more and more accounts were made known, it had been apparent that they were true. Finally the rancher whose wife had been raped, Miles Gillett, came forward to say that he had proof the culprit was Clay Taggart. Ever since, every person toting a badge or wearing a uniform had had his eyes peeled for the renegade. Whoever killed him would be famous.

The countryside through which the patrol traveled gradually changed from chaparral rife with manzanita to barren land, climbing steadily higher. Derrick was sure he would locate one of the renegade hideouts before the day was done, and he smiled in anticipation.

For three weeks the patrol had been making a routine sweep of the Chiricahua and Dragoons Mountains. For three weeks they had seen neither hide nor hair of a single, solitary renegade. And that was the way most patrols went. Ungodly long hours spent in the saddle under a blistering sun day after day after day, and for what?

But this time promised to be different. This time Capt. Derrick stood to become the envy of every officer in the Fifth Cavalry. In a year or so he'd make major, and from there the sky was the limit.

In the officer's excitement over being close to overtaking the White Apache, he failed to heed another piece of advice that Gerald Forester had once imparted.

"Watch your dust," the more experienced captain had said. "Thirty horses kick up a lot of it, especially at a full gallop. Apaches can see the cloud from miles off. So when you're closing in on some, be sure to go slow when you figure that you're close enough for them to spot you."

It had been sound advice, as Capt. Derrick would have realized had he been able to soar as high as the red hawk wheeling above his column and see the figures hidden behind boulders on a slope ahead.

Fiero, ever the most alert of the renegades, had seen the dust cloud first and pointed it out to the other warriors. He yipped a few times while waving his rifle, then cried, "It is a good day for white-eyes to die!"

Clay had studied the cloud a few moments, gauging distance and how fast the pursuers were moving. They had to be whites, since no self-respecting Apache would be so careless. He estimated the riders were three or four miles off and coming on at a gallop. Let them come! he mused. He would be ready.

Once, Clay Taggart would have balked at the notion of shooting soldiers who were only doing their duty. But that was before Gillett framed him, before Gillett manipulated the Army into doing what Gillett wanted done in the worst way. And since Clay had thrown in with the renegades, he had come to see things from the Apache point of view. He found himself siding with them against those who had forced the tribes to accept reservation life at gunpoint.

So on spying the dust, instead of feeling guilt at the idea of killing troopers, Clay Taggart felt outrage. Or, rather, the White Apache did. He thought and acted as a true Chiricahua, that part of him that was white buried by the part of him that had become Apache.

A talus slope dotted with boulders gave White Apache an inspiration. Veering to the right, he took a game trail up along the edge of the slope to the mountain above. The horse was unnerved by the narrow footing and the drop-off to one side. Several times White Apache had to jab his heels into its flanks to keep the animal climbing.

Marista, close behind, was also having trouble with the mare she rode, and not having been on a horse before she had no idea what to do. White Apache kept a close eye on her. When the mare suddenly stopped and refused to go on, he said, "We have to hurry. Use that pigsticker of yours and poke it in the rump. That ought to do the trick."

It did, but not in the way he had hoped. Marista pricked the horse lightly twice without result, so she jabbed it harder a third time. The animal's response caught her off guard. Without any warning whatsoever, the feisty mare bucked.

The Pima had one arm looped around her son, the reins held loosely in her left hand. She was nearly thrown by the violent motion, but by grabbing the saddle horn she hung on, her body swinging precariously to one side.

The mare landed with its legs straight, its back arched. The impact caused Marista to slip even more. She was poised above the talus slope, clinging for dear life. Another such jolt would send her plummeting.

White Apache reined up and slid off. Dashing to the mare, he grabbed the reins and held on tight. The animal tried to jerk back but he dug in his heels, buying time for Marista to scramble back into the saddle and get a good grip on the boy. Then, leading the mare, he held onto the end of the reins while mounting and pulled the animal along beside him to the top of the slope. There was scant cover save for a dry wash in which the horses were tied. They left the Pimas to keep watch.

White Apache led the warriors onto the slope. They fanned out, each seeking a sheltered nook. All five levered rounds into the chambers of their Winchesters.

Sprawled at the base of a boulder resembling a gigantic egg, White Apache braced his elbow on a smooth rock and scanned the terrain below, noting where there was cover for the soldiers and where there was not.

The dust cloud grew in size. Tiny stick figures appeared, becoming larger and larger as the range was narrowed.

White Apache adjusted the sights on his .44-40, setting them for one hundred yards. The 15-shot rifle had proven remarkably accurate at that range. Indeed, the Winchester Model 1873 was proving to be one of the most popular guns ever made, and there could be no greater testimony to its stopping power than the fact that every member of the band owned one. The rifles had been taken as part of the plunder from a wagon train.

Blood Treachery

The soldiers, White Apache knew, were armed with carbines, shorter versions of his rifle which were just as accurate but at a slightly shorter range.

At a swift clip the patrol approached. White Apache noticed a pair of Indian scouts at the head of the column. He couldn't tell which tribe they belonged to, but they definitely were not Apaches.

Presently the scouts drew rein and the young officer in charge raised his hand to halt the patrol. The officer conferred with them. Apparently a disagreement broke out, with the scouts shaking their heads and pointing repeatedly at the mountain. The officer overrode them. With an imperious gesture, he started them toward the talus slope and gave the order for the troopers to follow.

The scouts were uneasy, as well they should be. They held their rifles close to their chests so they could snap off shots at a moment's notice.

White Apache almost felt sorry for them. They suspected the patrol was riding into an ambush but the officer wanted to push on anyway. It served them right for turning against other Indians, for hiring out to track down those whose only crime was in wanting to go on living as their ancestors had lived for generations, long before the coming of the whites.

A scout with a feather in his headband was slightly out in front. He raked the talus slope from top to bottom and side to side, his lanky frame curled so that most of his body was screened by the head and neck of his bay.

White Apache fixed a bead on the Indian's head, then changed his mind and swiveled to take aim at the cocky young officer. He waited, letting the patrol get closer, not about to fire until he was sure he couldn't miss. The others would wait for his signal.

Suddenly the Indian wearing the feather yanked on his reins, jabbed a finger at the slope, and cried out in alarm.

The words were indistinct but the meaning was clear. The scout had caught sight of one of the Apaches or else seen sunlight glimmer off a rifle barrel. Immediately the officer rose in his stirrups and snapped a hand into the air to halt the cavalrymen.

At that exact moment White Apache fired. He had fixed his sights on the officer's chest and would have killed the man then and there had the officer not risen. As it was, the shot took the trooper low in the stomach and punched him off his mount.

All hell broke loose.

The renegades opened up with a vengeance, the warriors firing as rapidly as they could work the levers of their Winchesters. Simultaneously, the troopers charged, all except for a noncom and two others who rushed to the aid of the stricken officer. Spreading to either flank, the soldiers fired their carbines at random. The couldn't see the renegades, but they could see the puffs of gunsmoke that told them where the warriors were hidden.

Slugs whined off boulders, ricocheting wildly. White Apache pressed his face to the ground as a firestorm of lead chewed up the earth around him. Rising up again, he shot a soldier out of the saddle, then winged another in the shoulder.

The boom of guns was deafening. Added to the din was the lusty curses of the soldiers, the strident war whoops of the Apaches, and the frightened nickers of cavalry mounts.

In the midst of this bedlam, White Apache kept his head. He fired methodically, picking targets with care, never wasting lead. And since the troopers would be virtually helpless without their mounts, he shot as many horses as he did men.

The soldiers were fearless and determined and they outnumbered their foes by five to one, but they were out in the open, racing headlong into a withering rain of bullets that no living thing could withstand. Men and horses crumpled, some mortally stricken, some suffering minor wounds.

It was the noncom who rallied the survivors and got them out of there. Bellowing like a madman, he regrouped the shattered detachment and retreated to the south, the wounded being helped by their fellows.

Miraculously, neither of the scouts was hit. At the outbreak of gunfire they had slipped onto the sides of their animals, Comanche fashion, and fled while hanging by one arm and leg. Not until they were well out of range did they straighten and stop to await the soldiers.

White Apache rose as the last of the troopers sped off into the swirling dust. He sighted on the back of one of the men and was about to squeeze the trigger when he had an abrupt change of heart. For a fleeting moment some of Clay Taggart asserted itself, some of the white man who had been reared on a ranch and taught that only cowards shot others in the back.

Lowering the Winchester, White Apache stepped around the boulder. Fiero and Ponce, howling like wolves in the grip of bloodlust, were bounding down the talus slope. Delgadito and Cuchillo Negro had risen but did not join them.

Turning, White Apache headed for the ridge to check on the Pimas. At the crown he glanced back and saw the firebrand and the young warrior mutilating a soldier. Fiero had gutted the body and was gleefully waving the slimy intestines in the air.

Marista and Colletto were near the horses. She gave White Apache a long, searching look, then reached out to touch his left arm. "You be hit."

A slug had creased him, breaking the skin and drawing blood but doing no real damage. White Apache shrugged. "It's a scratch. Nothing to get concerned about." He faced the battleground. "Now you see why hooking up with me is downright dangerous. The soldiers want me dead in the worst way, and they won't rest until they bring me down."

"I not care. We stay with you."

White Apache felt her hand slip into his. She squeezed and he did the same. Then, as he was about to peck her on the cheek, he saw the boy glance sharply at the crest. Letting go, he discovered that Delgadito and Cuchillo Negro had arrived.

The former was delighted by the outcome. "This was a great victory! When the warriors in the village hear, they will flock to our cause." He screeched for joy. "The white-eyes never learn. Again and again we send them running with their tails between their legs, and still they try to stop us."

"This was a little skirmish, nothing more," White Apache disputed him. "Whipping one measly patrol doesn't mean a thing. They'll go back to their post to report, and before you know it we'll have patrols combing every square inch of this country."

"Let them," Delgadito said. "They will never find us."

Confidence was fine, but it was White Apache's opinion that his mentor had a little too much. A fine line existed between faith in one's ability and arrogance, and once that line was crossed the offender frequently paid a heavy price. "I don't know, pard," he said. "Those two scouts knew their business. It wouldn't surprise me if they show up again real soon."

"Cibicues," Delgadito said in disdain. "They are skilled, but not skilled enough. We will conceal our trail in case they come back."

"There is the matter of their guns," Cuchillo Negro reminded them.

Every last body was stripped of weapons and ammunition, which were loaded onto the pack horses. White Apache resumed their trek with Marista at his side while the four warriors lingered to wipe out their tracks.

There was a technique to it. Using a bush or a limb to brush away every last print wasn't enough. The brush marks themselves had to be covered with a fine layer of loose dirt so that the ground appeared perfectly natural. Rocks had to be strategically placed. Apaches were masters of the art, and within twenty minutes the Chiricahuas had caught up with the horses.

White Apache noticed the boy secretly eyeing him and figured Colletto was taking his measure. The youngster rarely spoke and acted awed by all that had occurred.

Having the sprout and the woman to look after gave Clay a lot to think about. Another lifetime ago he had longed to have a family, to marry Lilly and raise a passel of young ones, a brood to carry on the Taggart name. That dream had been dashed the day Lilly betrayed him, but every so often he would recall those days and wish his dream might still come to pass.

Toward evening, in the middle of some of the starkest, most rugged landscape Clay had ever seen, Delgadito jogged up next to his horse and pointed at an isolated spire to the northeast, a needle of rock thrusting skyward as if in defiance.

"Eagle's Roost, *Lickoyee-shis-inday*. We will be there before the night is half done."

"Fine by me," Clay responded. "The woman and boy are plumb wore out. The rest will do them good." Stretching, he commented, "I just hope this place is as safe as Cuchillo Negro claims. I don't want the cavalry to show up."

Delgadito turned somber. "It is not the cavalry you need to worry about. It is the *Gans*."

Chapter Nine

His name was Gian-nah-tah and he was in the prime of his life, a strapping, robust young man of twenty winters whose sole ambition was that of most young men his age. It had to do with a woman.

Gian-nah-tah had long coveted the daughter of Soldado, a radiant beauty whose name meant Corn Watcher. To him, she had the most lustrous hair and vibrant form of any woman in the tribe. At night he dreamed of her, tossing and turning in fervent desire. During the day he dreamed of her too, and often he could not resist sneaking close to her father's lodge so he could admire her without being seen.

Gian-nah-tah was in love, although he would never admit as much. For an Apache warrior to admit to such weakness was demeaning. He told no one, but almost everyone knew, including the father of the *ninya*, who one day encountered the young warrior by chance and said that which stunned Gian-nah-tah so much, his tongue seemed to go numb.

"You want my daughter."

Soldado waited for a reply, and when none was forthcoming, he went on. "It is no secret. Just as it is no secret she has other suitors, warriors who have proven themselves time and again. What do you have to offer her?"

Gian-nah-tah had nothing to say, for in truth he had the clothes on his back and the rifle in his hand and that was it. He had not yet taken a wife, so he still lived in the wickiup of his father.

"It is true Palacio is your uncle, and he thinks highly of you," Soldado continued, "but his praise will not put food in my daughter's belly or help make the hard work women must do any easier for her to bear."

"This is so," Gian-nah-tah finally blurted.

"I will be honest with you," Soldado said. "Corn Watcher prefers you over all her other suitors, and she longs for the day you will bring your horse to our lodge so she might lead it to water." His pause was much longer than it needed to be. "But you do not have a horse yet, do you?"

Gian-nah-tah was too crestfallen to answer.

"I have raised my daughter to make a good wife. She is healthy, strong, a virgin. She could have any man she wanted, but she wants you." Again the father paused. "If you want her, prove yourself worthy of the prize. If you do not, I will forbid her to go to you. You have four moons to show me her trust is justified."

The young warrior had watched the older one walk off in mixed elation and dismay. He was thrilled to learn that the woman he cherished cared for him, but he was shattered by the ultimatum. How was he to prove himself in so short a time? Stealing a few horses would not be enough. He needed to do something more spectacular, something that would show everyone he was worthy.

Then came the meeting Palacio called, and Gian-nah-tah was surprised to find himself invited along with four of the most influential men in the tribe. Only when he heard of the offer made by the white-eyes did he understand.

His uncle Palacio knew of his talk with Soldado. Palacio was trying to help him, giving him a chance to earn Soldado's respect and Corn Watcher's hand by allowing him to get a head start on other warriors who might be inclined to turn in the renegades for the bounty.

That very night Gian-nah-tah borrowed his father's stallion and left the village to begin his search. First he traveled to Sweet Grass, which was deserted, and from there to several other remote places known only to the Chiricahuas. At each and every one he met with disappointment.

A new day dawned. Gian-nah-tah rose early and made off toward Rabbit Ears. He could think of two or three other spots that deserved attention, and he would not rest until he had checked them all.

As the young warrior rode along with the warm wind blowing his long black hair, he happened to gaze to the northeast and spied in the far distance the spire known as Eagle's Roost. He remembered the cave there, which he had seen once as a small boy. Briefly he considered making a detour but he dismissed the idea. Eagle's Roost was the haunt of an evil mountain spirit. Everyone knew that. Not even the renegades would dare go there.

Or would they?

Torn by indecision, Gian-nah-tah pressed on toward Rabbit Ears. Perhaps he would go check Eagle's Roost another time. Perhaps not.

Marista's laughter dazzled Clay Taggart. He sat propped on his saddle near the spring in the spacious cave they now called home and watched as she skinned a rattlesnake Colletto had killed. There was no squeamishness on her part. She went about the task with cheerful precision, cutting and slicing so quickly that her hands flew.

"Tell me more about your people," Clay urged.

Marista had been explaining how her tribe diverted water from the Salt and Gila Rivers to irrigate the soil for farming. She had mentioned that as a very little girl she had often jumped naked into the ditches to splash and play on hot days, and Clay had replied that there was a sight he would like to see. Which sparked her mirth.

"Pimas have two clans," she revealed. "White Ant people and Red Ant people. I be White Ant."

"Where are your antennae?"

She looked up, puzzled. *"Neh?"*

Clay put his hands to his head and waved two fingers around and around. "Antennae," he said, grinning.

Marista chuckled heartily. Her cares and woes had been forgotten for the moment; she appeared ten years younger. "My father White Ant. His father White Ant. His father also White Ant."

"I get the idea," Clay said, and absently asked, "Couldn't your pa help you when your husband wanted to kick you out?" The sorrow it provoked made him regret his blunder and he hastily added, "Sorry. I reckon I have the brains of a mule."

"Father no can help," Marista said sadly.

Desperate to change the subject, Clay observed the Apaches huddled at the cave mouth and thought of their superstition regarding the *Gans*. "Tell me. Do your people believe in the Almighty? In God? Or in Yusn, as the Chiricahuas call him?"

She brightened. "Pimas believe two gods. Earthgiver and Elder Brother."

"Never heard that one before," Clay admitted. "How about evil spirits? The Apaches put a lot of store in them."

"Yes. There be Evil Spirit over all."

Clay stared into the pool and saw his likeness reflected. "Makes a man wonder," he said. "If so many different people believe in one, there must be one." He dipped a hand in the water and raised a mouthful to his lips.

"Delicious, yes? That right word?"

"It sure is," Clay said. "Which reminds me. Where did you learn to speak the white man's tongue?"

Marista stopped peeling the skin from the snake. She pronounced her next words slowly and distinctly. "From Doctor David Wooster of San Francisco. You know him?"

"Heard of him," Clay replied. Wooster had lived among the Pimas for quite some time, tending their sick and doing what little he could to raise their standard of living. The physician had grown warmly attached to the Pimas and was still spoken of highly by them even though several years had gone by since he left for California.

"He heal mother when she sick. Heal many Pimas. White Ant, Red Ant, all be same to him."

Clay wondered what motivated people like the good doctor. He didn't see how anyone could be so selfless and devoted to easing human misery, the world being the way it was. It had been his experience that most folks would as soon stab another in the back as look at them. He was a prime example. Lilly had turned on him, Gillett had tried to have him lynched, the Army was after him for taking revenge on the backstabbers who had strung him up. Simple decency and goodness were dying out, and soon the human race wouldn't have a shred of either. As for justice, there was none in the world unless it was the justice dispensed by the business end of a pistol or rifle.

Just then Delgadito called out, breaking Clay's train of thought. "*Lickoyee-shis-inday*. Come see."

Rising, Clay hastened over and crouched beside the warriors. They were staring at a lone figure moving across the wasteland far to the southwest, a figure so distant it was the size of an ant, a tiny speck moving along against the brown backdrop of parched countryside.

"One man on horseback," Delgadito said.

"A *Shis-Inday*," Fiero added.

Clay squinted but could not distinguish a single detail. "How can you be sure it is an Apache?" he asked.

"I am sure," the firebrand declared. "He is heading for Rabbit Ears, where we stayed two moons ago."

"Could it be an Army scout hunting for us?" Clay questioned.

Fiero leaned forward. "No, he does not wear a blue coat. Perhaps he is a hunter in search of antelope." He wagged his rifle in the figure's direction. "I will go see who it is, if you want."

Blood Treachery

"He might spot you," Clay said. "It is best if no one knows where we are, not even other Chiricahuas. So I say we should let him go his way in peace."

No one objected, which Clay took as a good sign. There had been a time when they argued every time he opened his mouth. Moving to the very brink of the ledge fronting the cave, he surveyed the area.

Eagle's Roost was aptly named. Two-thirds of the way up the stone spire was an old nest built by eagles a long time ago in a niche in the rock surface. It wasn't being used, so either the eagles had aged and died or been killed.

About a hundred feet below the nest, the spire flared to a wide base. Here the cave was situated. It measured some eighty feet across and forty feet from front to back, including the pool, which was six feet in diameter.

A narrow trail, barely the width of two moccasins, wound from the cave mouth to the canyon floor below, a distance of approximately three-hundred feet. Brush and a few trees grew in the canyon, and in one of those sparse stands the horses were secreted.

In Clay's opinion, it was the ideal hideout. Water was there for the taking, game could be had with effort, and the cave was so far off the beaten path that the odds of anyone stopping by any time soon were remote. For the time being they were safe. They did not have to keep looking over a shoulder every minute of every day. They could relax, really and truly relax.

Fiero let out with a long sigh. "I, for one, do not like all this sitting around. We are warriors, not women. We should be off raiding the Mexicans or one of the white-eyes who hanged White Apache."

"We will soon enough," Clay said. "Be patient."

Fiero grunted. Everyone knew that of all the Chiricahuas, he was the least patient. "If I cannot kill enemies, I will kill something for our supper pot." So saying, the burly warrior stepped to the trail and descended.

Clay opened his mouth to call him back but stopped when Cuchillo Negro placed a hand on his shoulder.

"Always remember, my friend, that Apaches are free to do as they want. You cannot hold Fiero here against his will. If he wants to hunt, he can."

"He might give our hiding place away," Clay complained. "Is it right that all of us suffer because he does not know how to be patient?"

Cuchillo Negro countered the query with one of his own. "Is it for us you are so worried, or for them?" He pointed at the Pimas.

Ponce had risen and was inspecting the cave floor and one wall. "Look at all this dust," he remarked. "No one has stayed here since the death of Toga-de-chuz."

"His bones should be here somewhere," Cuchillo Negro said.

"Unless the mountain spirit ground them to dust," Delgadito mentioned.

Peeved that Fiero had gone off, Clay was in no mood to talk about their silly superstition. He walked back to the spring and sat down close to Marista, who took one look at him and asked, "Something be wrong?"

"No. I'm fine," Clay said. No sooner did he speak than an inexplicable shiver ran down his spine. He faced the opening, thinking the wind had kicked up, but the air was sluggish. For a few brief moments he had the eerie feeling that unseen eyes were upon him. He scanned the dark walls and ceiling, feeling foolish doing so, but saw nothing out of the ordinary.

Nerves, Clay reckoned. A case of bad nerves was all it was, spawned by Fiero going off by his lonesome. One day soon the hothead was going to get them all into a heap of trouble. He just knew it.

Col. Reynolds was buried in paperwork at his desk when the orderly rapped on the office door and announced that Capt. Forester wanted to see him. "Show him in," the colonel said, setting down his quill pen.

Gerald Forester was in a huff, as the flinty cast of his features revealed. He marched up to the desk and stood at attention until told to stand at ease.

"What's the prognosis?" Colonel Reynolds inquired.

"The surgeon says that with a little luck, Derrick will pull through, sir. He'll be laid up for two months, possibly longer. And he'll never be the man he was before. But he'll be alive, which I suppose is some consolation."

"Why so cynical, Captain?"

Forester ran his fingers along his sweeping mustache and tweaked one end. "It's this whole White Apache business, sir. The man is a butcher. He deserves to be stood in front of a firing squad."

"I couldn't agree more."

"Then why won't you let me go after him?" Forester clenched his fists. "I know that country well, sir. Sgt. Bryce told me exactly where the ambush took place. The Flying Detachment can be there in two days if we limit ourselves to four hours of sleep each night. We might be able to catch Taggart, at long last."

"Might, Captain. Might," Reynolds said severely. "No, I'm afraid my decision is final. The Flying Detachment does not leave Fort Bowie until we hear from Palacio."

"But sir," Forester said, forgetting himself and gripping the edge of the desk, "with all due respect, I can't help thinking that you're making a grave mistake. You know as well as I do that Headquarters has made the capture or slaying of the White Apache a top priority. And we may never get a better chance. My men and I are ready. Say the word and I'll bring the son of a bitch back draped over a saddle."

Reynolds folded his hands in his lap and sat back. "I appreciate your zeal, Captain. However, I can't help wondering if it stems from our standing orders or your longstanding friendship with Captain Derrick." The Colonel sighed and gazed out the window. "As for missing an opportunity, I doubt that's the case. Clay Taggart has proven to be quite shrewd. He's not about to stick around the site of an ambush. And since it took Bryce four days to get here after the attack, by the time you reach the area almost a whole week will have gone by. Hell, man. Taggart could be in Canada by then."

Captain Forester straightened. He reluctantly had to admit that his superior had a valid point. He had allowed his friendship for Henry Derrick to sway his judgment. "You're right, of course, sir. I'm sorry I bothered you. May I be excused?"

Reynolds hesitated. He liked Forester more than most of his subordinates. The man was a topnotch soldier and one of the few genuinely dedicated officers he had ever met. Most, himself included, were more interested in merely putting in their twenty years and leaving the military with a modest pension to see them through their golden years. Forester couldn't be bothered with counting the days until his retirement. The man was actually devoted to his country, to serving in the best capacity he knew how.

"As my dear, departed grandmother used to say to me when I was knee high to a colt and always acting up, you must possess your soul in patience, Captain. The wheels have been set in motion. It's only a matter of time before one of the Chiricahuas learns where the renegades are hiding out. Then you'll get your wish."

"I can hardly wait, sir."

Fiero had not earned his name for nothing. He had a temperament that blazed as hot as the sun when he was angry or upset, and he was upset now. Hiding out in a cave wasn't his idea of how to wage war on the despicable white-eyes who had stolen Chiricahua land right out from under the tribe. It would take many raids, and many Americans would have to die before the chiefs of the whites would give thought to leaving the territory. White Apache had told him as much.

Thinking of *Lickoyee-shis-inday* only made Fiero more upset. Begrudgingly, he had grown to like White Apache, to regard him as a full-fledged member of the band. Then the man went and did something like this, bringing them to a cave inhabited by an evil mountain spirit just so the Pimas would be safe!

It was added proof that, just as Fiero had long maintained, women were a burden. They made strong men weak. They clouded the judgment of those caught in their spell. It was why Fiero would never take a wife. He was pledged to resist the white invaders until the day he died, if need be, and he would not let any female weaken his resolve.

Delgadito had been weak once, Fiero mused, and the result had been disastrous. It was Delgadito who had insisted on taking women and children into Mexico when the band splintered off from Palacio's followers. "We cannot leave behind those who depend on us for their welfare," Delgadito had claimed.

Noble sentiments, but impractical. The band had not been able to travel very fast with so many women and children to watch over. It had enabled the scalphunters to catch them when and where they were most vulnerable. Few would ever know how close the band came to being exterminated that day.

Fiero had not been there, but he had seen the aftermath. He had stood on the rim of the hollow in which the massacre had taken place, and he had felt as if his insides were being ripped apart.

The slaughter had been horrendous. Women had been shot to shreds as they fled with infants in their arms. Small children had been sliced wide open, their innards left hanging from their bloated bellies for the scavengers to feast on. And every last one had been scalped.

It mattered little to Fiero that later White Apache had led the band into Mexico and tracked down the scalphunters who were to blame. He had learned his lesson. Never again would he entangle himself with women and young ones. Yet here he was, doing just that because of White Apache.

Scowling, Fiero paused to take control of his

emotions. A warrior must never let his mind wander, he reminded himself, and raised his nose to the wind to test for the scent of game, or enemies. Turning, he saw Eagle's Roost far off, the mouth of the cave like a black spot on the stone spire. There was no sign of the others, which was to be expected. They had grown foolish but not that foolish.

A little farther on, Fiero came on fresh deer tracks left by a doe and a fawn that had passed that way earlier in the day. He trailed them, jogging tirelessly into the gathering twilight. A promise was a promise, and he had said that he would bring meat for the cooking pot.

Perhaps because Fiero was upset, or because of his promise, or because it was growing late and he wanted to return to the cave before it was too dark to track, he hurried on, giving no thought to his own tracks.

No thought at all.

The sun had not yet rimmed the eastern horizon when Gian-nah-tah swung onto his father's stallion and headed eastward from Rabbit Ears. The renegades had not been there. No one had in quite some time. His list of possible places to check was growing shorter by the day, and with each waning moon he stood in greater jeopardy of losing Corn Watcher.

Gian-nah-tah had not eaten in a day and a half. His stomach rumbled constantly but he paid it no heed. He would eat after he located the renegades, not before.

Leaving the twin peaks behind, Gian-nah-tah set off across a flat plain into a region of twisted gullies and steep canyons. He was riding with his chin low, depressed at the prospect of losing the woman he wanted to another warrior, when the strong scent of spilled blood made him snap up and look around.

Sixty feet away lay the carcass of a dead deer. The young warrior rode over, expecting to find a cougar kill. Instead, he discovered a butchered doe and fawn. The doe had been dropped by a single shot to the head. The fawn had had its throat slit when it refused to leave its mother. Only the doe had been skinned, and most of the choice meat was gone.

Gian-nah-tah sat on the stallion and tingled all over. Not because of the doe. He had slain scores of them himself. Nor because of the fawn, even though its death had been needless. No, he tingled because of the tracks in the dirt beside the deer.

The tracks of the warrior who had killed them.

The tracks of an Apache warrior.

Of a Chiricahua.

And they made off straight toward Eagle's Roost.

Chapter Ten

Palacio was astride his finest horse and dressed in his finest clothes. He had a new Bowie knife strapped to his ample middle, received in trade from the same two smugglers who had sold him the three rifles he kept hidden under a pile of blankets in his lodge.

Riding with the Chiricahua leader were his nephew, old Nantanh, Juan Pedro, and Chico. Palacio had brought the last three along so they could see for themselves the esteem in which the white-eyes held him. And to be sure he was treated with the respect that was his due, he had sent a messenger on ahead to inform White Hair that they were coming.

Palacio smiled in delight when one of the *soldados* high on the stone lodge saw him and bellowed for all to hear.

"It's the chief! Open the gate!"

For the benefit of the others, Palacio translated.

He took the liberty of embellishing a little by adding the word "great" before chief, and then said, "See? It is because the white-eyes hold me in such high regard that I can do much good for our people."

"Since when is it good for Chiricahua to betray Chiricahua?" Nantanh asked with a pointed glare at Gian-nah-tah.

"Would you rather live at San Carlos?" Palacio retorted, beginning to regret that he had invited the venerable warrior. The old fool had groused the whole trip, sniping at Palacio for allowing such treachery. "That is where we will end up if the White Apache and the misguided men with him are not stopped."

Juan Pedro grunted agreement. "San Carlos is for those who want to live like dogs. Chiricahuas do not go around on all fours."

Nantanh was not cowed. "I, too, hate the idea of being forced to live with tribes who have been our enemies longer than any man can remember. But the white-eyes are no better, despite what Palacio claims. They use us to their own ends. Just as they use us now to do that which they have not been able to do in all the moons Delgadito has waged war against them."

Palacio was glad when the huge gate creaked inward. It shut the old fool up so he could lead them on in, his head high. To his surprise, White Hair had arranged a reception.

Twenty troopers in clean uniforms stood in a long line, polished rifles at their sides. At the head of the line was White Hair himself, holding a gleaming long-knife. At his command, the soldiers presented arms, and all activity in the fort ceased as all eyes swung toward the visitors.

Giddy at this tribute to his importance, Palacio

beamed at the row of soldiers as his horse pranced past them. To a man, they gazed straight ahead, as motionless as a row of trees.

Unknown to Palacio, the reception had been Capt. Gerald Forester's idea, not Col. Reynold's. On being called into the commander's office the day before to receive word of the impending visit, Forester had remarked, "Maybe you should roll out the honor guard. The fat bastard loves it when he's treated like royalty. It makes him easier to deal with."

Now, watching Palacio act like some sort of foreign potentate from the front porch of the main building, Capt. Forester nudged Sgt. McKinn and said out of the corner of his mouth, "I swear, if that head of his swells any bigger, it'll go floating off like a balloon." The noncom, who hated Apaches with a passion, snickered.

Neither was aware that Col. Reynolds overheard the comment but overlooked it. Stepping around in front of the honor guard, Reynolds performed a left moulinet with his saber, then a right moulinet, then slid the saber into its scabbard and offered a salute. He could not but notice the look Palacio gave the other warriors, and he realized that Forester had the man's character pegged.

"Greeting, friend," Reynolds stated. "Climb down. I have everything set up so we can get right to business." He indicated the side of the building, where blankets and stools had been set out for the council.

Palacio slid off his horse, smoothed his frilly blue shirt, and extended his hand in the white manner. "I am happy to see you again, White Hair. But you did not need to do all this for me."

The false humility was thick enough to be cut with a knife. Reynolds took it in stride and shook. For a man whose body resembled whale blubber, the chief was immensely strong. "I have looked forward to this day with relish. At long last the White Apache will be brought to account for his many crimes."

"Once you learn where he is."

Something in the Chiricahua's tone bothered Reynolds. "You did find out? That is the reason you came?"

"Oh, most assuredly," Palacio said, his grin as slick as that of a saloon cardsharp. "And, as we agreed, the information will be yours in exchange for the bounty you offered." He made a show of surveying the compound. "As I recall, there was mention of eight horses, forty blankets, six knives, an axe, and tobacco. Yet I do not see them."

Reynolds was anxious to send the Flying Detachment on its way. Any delay could prove costly; Taggart might elect to go somewhere else. But short of throttling the information out of Palacio, there was nothing he could do but play along and hope the devious savage didn't keep him waiting all damn day.

"A quick visit to the stable and the sutler's and you'll have all the bounty I promised you," Reynolds said.

Palacio lumbered toward the blankets. "Not too quick, I trust? I am thirsty after my long ride. And I have been thinking the whole time of my last visit, my friend, and those scrambled eggs you shared with me."

Col. Reynolds turned to his adjutant. "You heard the man. Have a pitcher of water brought. And tell the cook I want heaping portions of scrambled eggs out here in ten minutes."

"Do not forget some sweet cakes," Palacio said. He licked his thick lips. "I do so love those wonderful sweet cakes you have for your morning meal."

There were times, Col. Reynolds reflected, when he swore it would be easier dealing with Delgadito.

Clay Taggart had the nightmare on the seventh night the band stayed at Eagle's Roost. In it he was fleeing on foot from a large number of troopers who peppered the air with hot lead. He had his rifle and he fired as he ran, but to his amazement the bullets bounced off the soldiers. They gained rapidly. Just when he thought they would run him down, he spied a cave. Darting into its dark depths, he fired at the horses of his pursuers, dropping five or six before the soldiers scattered to take cover. He congratulated himself on his narrow escape and took stock.

The cave was huge, so huge Clay couldn't see the ceiling or tell how far underground it extended. There was a spring, though, which meant he could hold out indefinitely. Kneeling to take a drink, he heard a scraping noise overhead and looked up to see a pair of blazing red eyes the size of saucers fixed on him.

Startled, Clay cried out and tried to bring the rifle up. Before he could, a vague black shape swept down and caught him its in grip. The thing was monstrous, with the shape and consistency of a wet blanket and the power of a bull buffalo. Clay was helpless in its iron grasp. Little by little the life was being crushed from his body while those awful red eyes glared into his and hot, fetid breath fanned his face.

Clay's ribs shattered, popping like fireworks one after the other. He opened his mouth to scream and the creature's own gaping maw yawned wide. Out of it shot a vile, slimy black tongue that rolled down Clay's throat, piercing his vitals. He struggled mightily, thrashing and kicking, but it was to no avail.

With a last, Herculean effort Clay tried to break free. He managed to straighten, and suddenly found himself seated on the smooth floor of the cave, his body caked with sweat. Something covered his mouth. He clutched at it and grabbed a slender wrist.

Soft lips brushed his ear. "You be all right, Clay. You have bad dream."

Slowly Clay came to his senses. His body gave a convulsive shake and he gently pried her hand away. Gulping in the cool night air, he whispered, "I'm obliged."

"You cry out in sleep. Why?"

Clay wondered the same thing. He glanced at the ceiling, then at the walls, which were plunged in inky darkness. No piercing red eyes glared back at him, but he had that strange sensation again of being watched by someone unseen. It was downright spooky. "Maybe something I ate didn't agree with me," he fibbed.

The warriors slept soundly over near the cave mouth. About six feet away Colletto snored lightly.

Clay mopped his brow with the back of his hand and laid back down. Marista snuggled beside him, resting her head on his shoulder.

"You be troubled?"

What should he tell her? Clay mused. That he was letting some stupid superstition scare him silly? Or was there more to it than that? Was it a premonition of some sort? His ma had been a big believer in ghosts and spirits and such, which his pa had branded as so much nonsense. Clay had been partial to his father's way of thinking, but now he wondered.

"Clay?"

"I don't know what the dickens is wrong with me," Clay confessed. "But it might be smart to think about moving on. There must be somewhere else we can go where you and the boy will be safe."

"Chiricahuas be happy. They not like cave." Marista paused. "I not like much."

Clay shifted to face her. Their noses were tip to tip, her breath caressed his face. "You too? Then there's no doubt about it. I might be dense at times but I know when to take a blamed hint. We'll leave tomorrow after I palaver with the others about the best place to go."

Marista smiled.

The shadows highlighted her natural beauty, rendering her more sensual and alluring than any woman Clay had ever seen. It took his breath away, this beauty of hers, and before he could help himself he kissed her. Not a light kiss, either, which he had been prone to give in front of her son and the warriors. He kissed her passionately, all the ardor he had suppressed welling up out of him. It was the single greatest kiss of his entire life, and it seemed to last forever.

Then, as all such exquisite moments do, it came to an end. Marista stiffened and drew back.

Clay saw that she was looking over his shoulder, and half fearing she had seen the horrible red eyes of his nightmare, he spun. A husky shape loomed a few steps away. Clay started to reach for his Colt.

137

"Lickoyee-shis-inday, come quickly."

It was Fiero. Clay rose, snatched up his Winchester, and padded beside the warrior to the rim of the cave. He was taken aback to find all the Chiricahuas were awake and staring intently into the night. "What is it?" he asked.

"Listen," Delgadito said.

Clay did, but for the longest while he heard nothing other than the lonesome sigh of the wind and the occasional rustle of trees on the canyon floor. He was beginning to think his brother Apaches were imagining things when he heard a faint metallic clink. A few second later there was a sustained rattle.

They were sounds Clay recognized. Back in his ranching days he had delivered beef to area forts numerous times. He knew the many little sounds large bodies of soldiers made as they went about their daily routine, sounds exactly like these he was hearing. "Soldiers," he said.

"Many soldiers," Cuchillo Negro amended. "They left their horses far up the canyon and came the rest of the way on foot. They seek to block the trail to keep us from escaping."

"Then we must leave immediately," Clay declared, "before they realize that we know they are there."

"And before they find our horses," Cuchillo Negro said.

Delgadito motioned at the huge pile of smuggled goods, which had been placed against the left-hand wall. "We will have to leave the plunder, Lickoyee-shis-inday. It cannot be helped."

"Keep watch. I will be right back."

Clay hurried to the Pimas. Marista had roused her son and the pair were huddled next to the

138

spring. "Soldiers," he announced. "We have to skedaddle, pronto."

Marista paused just long enough to retrieve her water skin. She kept a firm grip on the boy and trailed Clay to the opening where the Apaches were streaking their faces and broad chests with dirt. Imitating them, Clay listened for more telltale noises from the canyon. It seemed awfully quiet down there now, too quiet for his liking.

Fiero stepped lightly to the narrow footpath. "I will go first," he volunteered. "Any white-eyes I see, I will slit their throats before they can cry out."

Clay worked the lever of his rifle. "If we should be separated," he whispered, "head due east. We will join up again at Council Rock."

As silently as a ghost, Fiero started down the ribbon of a path. He moved low to the ground, his body blending into the earth as if part of it. Delgadito waited a minute, then he followed.

Clay's turn was next. He took Marista's hand, she took Colletto's, and after bestowing a reassuring smile on both of them, he descended.

It had been easy to climb to the cave in broad daylight, when a person could see where to step. But in the murky gloom every stride was fraught with peril: a single misstep would result in tragedy. On either side there was a sheer drop of hundreds of feet, and at the bottom waited jagged boulders to dash the unwary to bits.

Clay avoided looking to right or left. Concentrating on the trail and nothing but the trail, he wound lower yard by precarious yard. Every now and then he did glance into the canyon but saw no sign of any troopers. He could only hope they were too busy getting into position to notice anything else. Twenty feet in front of him

Delgadito came to a bend and snaked around it surefootedly. He could no longer see Fiero, who had descended at a reckless rate.

There was an urgent tug on Clay's hand. Stopping, he twisted and was appalled to see that the boy had slipped and hung over the side. Marista's grip was all that kept Colletto from plummeting to his death.

Quickly Clay eased closer to her, leaned forward as far as he dared, and snagged the boy's wrist. Between the two of them they pulled Colletto high enough for him to regain his footing.

The boy's eyes were wide and his face pale, but to his credit he had not cried out when he fell nor uttered a sound while he dangled heartbeats from oblivion.

White Apache pressed Marista's shoulder, then moved on. Delgadito, unaware of the mishap, had more of a lead than before. White Apache looked over a shoulder and saw that Ponce had nearly overtaken them, while much farther back was Cuchillo Negro.

Resisting an urge to go faster than was prudent, White Apache slid one foot forward, then brought up the other leg, and repeated the process again and again. He tried to keep his mind on the matter at hand but his thoughts strayed.

Staying at Eagle's Roost had been a monumental blunder, and if he hadn't been so worried about the Pimas he would have seen the truth sooner. There was only the one way into and out of the cave, which offered no handy escape route in case of an emergency. And not being able to keep horses close by precluded a quick getaway.

Clay told himself that he should have listened to the Chiricahuas. As Delgadito had pointed out, there was no safe haven for them anywhere in Arizona. He had to accept that fact and deal with it.

Which brought up the issue that bothered Clay most of all: What should he do about Marista and Colletto? He yearned to keep them with him, but how could he do that if he couldn't find a spot where they could hide out without fear of being discovered by the Army or the law or bounty hunters? By staying with him, they would, in effect, be committing suicide. He couldn't let them do that.

Suddenly the breeze brought a low rustling noise that stopped as abruptly as it began. Clay stopped and strained but heard no more. He thought it might have been the sound of a struggle, perhaps Fiero dispatching a trooper. If so, other soldiers were bound to have also heard.

Hurrying on, White Apache came to the bend. As he edged around the curve, a sharp shout rent the night, punctuated by others, then a gun flashed and was answered in kind and suddenly the night pounded to the boom of manmade thunder.

Clay made no move to enter the fray. For one thing, he had no clear targets. For another, he was exposed and vulnerable, and more importantly so were the Pimas.

Then Ponce cut loose, firing at clusters of gun flashes on both sides of the canyon. Seconds later Cuchillo Negro joined in.

The soldiers could do the same, and did, loosing a staggered volley at the flame and smoke that belched from the rifles of the warriors. Many underestimated the range or shot wildly.

Slugs smacked into the path all around Clay, Marista, and Colletto or whizzed past their ears, so many that it seemed the sky rained lead. Clay had no choice but to return fire. He banged off several shots, turned, and urged, "Go back! Into the cave! It's our only chance!"

The woman complied, her son glued to her side. They reached Ponce, who back-pedaled up the incline and fired to cover them, but in doing so he drew more fire in their direction.

Afraid for their lives, Clay levered round after round, trying futilely to drive the soldiers to ground or at the very least make them slack off. There were just too many. He saw Delgadito hastening toward him and retreated. Of Fiero, there was no trace.

A shout rose above the thundering din, an officer, perhaps, who bellowed, "Keep firing, men! We've got them right where we want them!"

The man's meaning was plain. By forcing the band back into the cave, the cavalrymen would have the Chiricahuas trapped. The troopers could keep the band pinned down until the warriors weakened from lack of food or were all killed off.

Never in all Clay's life had he experienced such an unnerving ordeal. Bullets kept hitting the path or cleaving the air on either side. At any moment he dreaded one would hit Marista or Colletto and they would fall to their doom before he could catch them.

Clay had gone about halfway when a searing pain lanced his left arm. He looked down and saw a black furrow where the bullet had nicked him, blood trickling freely. Snapping the Winchester to his shoulder, he fired twice at gun flashes close to the base of the spire and thought he heard a shriek of pain. He worked the lever again and squeezed the trigger but this time a muted click told him the chamber was empty.

Reloading as he climbed, Clay saw Delgadito jerk to one side, totter, and lose his footing. He was certain the warrior would fall, but by flinging out a steely arm Delgadito caught hold of the edge of the footpath and saved himself temporarily. The warrior's other arm was pressed against his chest; he would not be able to hold on indefinitely.

"Hang on, pard!" Clay cried, and scurried to his friend's aid. The lead flew fast and furious. It was a miracle that neither of them was hit.

In moments Clay had yanked Delgadito onto the path. The warrior took but a second to tuck his wounded arm close to his chest, then they sped upward, Clay eager to rejoin the Pimas, Delgadito to avoid being shot again.

At last the cave materialized. Clay watched the Pimas slip into the shadows and gave a silent heartfelt thanks. If anything happened to her, he would never forgive himself for letting them become part of his life—a violent life certain to end in violent death. Cuchillo Negro and Ponce had flattened along the rim and were shooting methodically.

White Apache gained the entrance. He checked to verify Marista and her son were safely away from the rim, then went prone and added his Winchester to the unequal battle.

Grunting loudly, Delgadito crawled up over the edge and lay on his side, panting and grimacing. A large dark stain on his brown shirt marked where he had been hit. He tried to open his shirt to examine the wound but could not get his fingers to function.

Marista glided over, her water skin still at her

side. She glanced at Clay and said, "Should I?"

Not even hesitating, Clay answered, "Help him." It pleased him mightily that she had asked, for in doing so she gave added proof that she considered him to be her man and showed she would rely on his judgment where other men were concerned. At any other time he would have reveled in her devotion, but now he bent his cheek to the Winchester and was about to fire when the shooting below unexpectedly ended. The warriors promptly stopped firing.

Clay leaned back to collect his wits. It had all transpired so swiftly that only now could he fully appreciate the predicament they were in, which was summed up nicely by Ponce.

The youngest member of their band spat in disgust and bowed his chin to his chest. "I knew we should not have tempted the wrath of the *Gans*. Now we are dead men."

Chapter Eleven

Capt. Gerald Forester was fit to be tied.

Everything had gone smoothly until the Flying Detachment was almost in position, and then sheer bedlam had broken out. As a result, he had lost five good men, seasoned troopers cut down in the prime of their lives by the bullets of the renegades. Four of them, at any rate. The fifth man had been stabbed twice in the chest.

That in itself was disturbing, Forester reflected. It meant at least one of the Apaches had reached the valley floor before the firing broke out and must still be at large.

Now, with dawn mere minutes off and the situation stabilized, Forester had sent for those best suited to deal with whoever had slipped through his carefully laid net. Hearing a commotion, he looked up from the plate of cold beans he was wolfing and saw the answers to his problem approaching, all seven of them. Unfortunately, at their head tramped the biggest pain in the ass in the United States Army.

"You sent for me?" Capt. Vincent Parmalee said without ceremony.

"I sent for the scouts," Forester said.

"Who are under my command," Parmalee retorted. "Col. Reynolds was quite explicit on that point."

"As he was when he informed you that *I* would be in overall command."

Parmalee made no attempt to hide his spite. He resented being sent out with the Flying Detachment, resented being forced to follow the orders of a self-righteous stickler for rules and regulations like Forester, and resented being treated as if he were a worthless imbecile. "Where the scouts go, I go. So what can we do for you?"

Ignoring his fellow officer, Capt. Forester addressed Klo-sen. "Take all the scouts. Find the renegade who knifed Pvt. Confort. Bring me his head."

Parmalee sputtered, "Now see here!" But it was too late. Klo-sen had not waited for his approval but had turned and barked a single word that set all the scouts in motion. In no time they had vanished among the boulders and brush.

Captain Forester spooned more beans into his mouth. He had no use for Parmalee; the man was a waste of uniform. For the life of him he couldn't imagine why their superior had seen fit to send the sot along. In his estimation it was a pity the renegade hadn't knifed Parmalee instead of poor Pvt. Confort.

"I intend to file a protest with the colonel after we return to Fort Bowie," the Chief of Scouts snapped.

"You do that."

"Just because you were put in charge doesn't give you the right to ride roughshod over me. If for no other reason than common courtesy, you should clear all your orders to my scouts through me in advance. I don't like having you usurp my authority."

Forester set the plate down and stood. "If you're so damned upset about the scouts going off by themselves, there's a simple solution."

"There is?"

"Go with them," Forester suggested, knowing full well the man never would. Just as it was no secret that Parmalee drowned his troubles in a bottle, so was it no secret the man was an errant yellowbelly.

True to form, Parmalee sniffed and said, "I don't see where that's necessary. Besides, I'd never catch up to them." He walked off in a huff, saying over a shoulder, "I'll be working on my report to the colonel if you need me."

"I won't."

Outraged, Parmalee held his temper in check until he was safely behind a boulder the size of a buffalo. Then he vented his spleen in a series of blue oaths muttered nonstop. When that was done, he fumbled in his pocket for his silver flask, opened it, and greedily took several gulps. The alcohol burned his mouth and throat but he didn't care. To him it was the elixir of life, the balm of Gilead, the salvation of his frayed nerves.

Parmalee had been terrified when the battle erupted. Having been informed that they were close to the renegade stronghold, he had deliberately held his scouts to the rear of the column and then advanced at a snail's pace into the canyon. At the outbreak of gunfire, his scouts had dashed off to be in the thick of things, leaving him alone and defenseless, hiding behind a bush no bigger than a breadbasket. Several wild shots had nearly ended his life. One, in fact, had kicked dirt into his face, at which point he had come awfully close to soiling himself.

Shuddering at the memory, Parmalee took another sip, corked the flask, and slid it into his pants pocket. Squaring his shoulders, he started around the boulder, striding past a dry bush that rustled after he went by. Why it should rustle when there was no wind, he had no idea. It occurred to him to turn and look but he was too eager to get as far from the stone spire where the renegades were holed up to bother. At any moment another battle might break out, and he didn't care to be in the vicinity.

But just as Parmalee was about to walk out into the open, something clamped itself on his windpipe and he was drawn up short. Startled, he tried to cry out and reached up to find an iron forearm looped around his neck. It shocked him so badly that he froze, and the next instant felt an agonizing spasm in his abdomen, a spasm that rippled higher, deep into his chest, and choked off the breath in his throat.

The arm was withdrawn.

Parmalee felt a warm, sticky sensation creeping down over his stomach and thighs. He glanced down and his knees turned to water at the horrifying sight he beheld. His stomach had been sliced clean open, his uniform and flesh sheared as neatly as you please by a blade so sharp he had been disemboweled in the blink of an eye.

It couldn't be! Parmalee told himself even as rock hard hands seized him by the back of the shirt and flung him to the earth at the base of the boulder. A swarthy face bearing a scar in the shape of a lightning bolt on its brow appeared above him and dark, fiery eyes regarded him with blatant contempt. Softly spoken words fell on his ears, but he did not understand them.

"Pindah lickoyee das-ay-go, dee-dah tatsan."

Parmalee tried to answer but his vocal chords were paralyzed. The face disappeared and he felt hands stripping him of his revolver and personal effects. In a little while the face reappeared, studying the flask. He saw the savage take a swig, grimace, and toss the whiskey aside. Then the Apache was gone.

Shocked to his core, growing weaker by the moment, Capt. Vincent Parmalee gazed at the heavens with eyes moistened by tears. It wasn't fair. He hadn't wanted to be there. He had done his best to avoid combat. And look at what had happened! He had one last thought before the world turned inside out and a yawning black pit swallowed him up, one last thought that summed up his existence as succinctly as any epitaph:

Life made no damn sense.

Fiero slipped off soundlessly, conforming the shape and motion of his body to the terrain. He hadn't intended to kill again so soon, but he could not pass up the opportunity to rub out a little chief of the white-eyes. Thanks to White Apache, he knew how to tell the chiefs from the soldiers under them by the strange braids on the shoulders of their uniforms.

It amazed Fiero that the white-eye had not realized he was there. The man had practically stepped on top of him. But then, every Chiricahua knew that the whites had senses as keen as a two-day old infant.

Like all Apache warriors, Fiero had learned at an early age how to move without making noise, how to blend into the landscape so that he was virtually invisible. By the age of eight, he had been able to imitate a bush or a boulder so expertly that no one could tell he was there. His father had also taught him how to dig a shallow depression in which to hide and then cover himself lightly with loose dirt. Plus many other tricks that had saved his skin time and time again.

Now Fiero was bearing to the southeast. He planned to swing wide around the soldiers and see how close he could get to Eagle's Roost. There had to be something he could do to help the rest of the band, although he had no idea what it might be. He did not like to think of the fact that some of them might be dead.

In his mind's eye Fiero reviewed the battle. He recalled descending the footpath well ahead of the others only to find the area swarming with troopers. Flattening, he had tried to crawl through their lines undetected, but an unwitting idiot had stumbled on him and he had stabbed the man to keep him from shouting. Unfortunately, nearby soldiers had heard, and the next thing Fiero knew, the night was ablaze with gunfire. He had done what he could to keep the troopers away from the base of the footpath so that his companions could reach the bottom in safety, but the odds had been hopeless. He had been forced to give ground to save his own life and had hidden close at hand, watching the whites, until the little chief nearly stepped on him.

Pausing, Fiero looked back to gauge how far he was from the enemy line. The soldiers had formed a partial ring around the great stone spire, with most of them concentrated near the footpath. Others had taken possession of the horses left secreted in the trees and added them to the string of cavalry mounts, which were under guard.

Fiero saw that he was several hundred yards from where the horses were tethered. He also saw that which brought a savage smile to his lips. Several Army scouts were advancing swiftly in his direction. One had his face to the ground, reading sign. Whoever he was, the man was very good. He was right on Fiero's trail.

High on the spire, Clay Taggart paced like a caged animal, racking his brain for a way out of the fix the band was in. He moved a step nearer to the rim to peek down at the troopers and had to jump back when a slug bit off slivers of stone from the edge.

It had been that way since shortly before dawn. Evidently the soldiers wanted to keep anyone from firing down at them, so whenever one of the troopers saw so much as a flickering shadow, he fired. So far the shots had struck the mouth of the cave and whined harmlessly off.

Clay gnawed his lower lip and pondered. Marista and the boy were by the spring, fixing breakfast. There had been a parfleche of venison jerky among the effects belonging to the smugglers, as well as coffee and flour.

Delgadito lay close to the small crackling fire. His side had been bandaged with torn strips from his own shirt and he was resting comfortably enough. The bullet had gouged a deep furrow in his side, chipping part of a rib bone, cracking another, and exiting low on his back, making a hole the size of a human fist. His organs had been spared but he had lost a terrible amount of blood.

Cuchillo Negro and Ponce squatted just back from the rim, rifles across their thighs. Neither had spoken or even moved in quite a while.

Clay slapped his leg in irritation and said in the Chiricahua tongue, "There has to be way to beat the white-eyes. We cannot let them keep us penned in here. Our food will only last a few days."

"We have water," Ponce said.

"Which helps, but will not keep us alive for long after the food is gone," Clay stressed. Staring at the rear of the cave, he said, "Are all of you certain there is no other way down from here? Have you looked to see if there is a passage?"

Delgadito had been listening attentively. "We were told there is none so we have never searched." Rising onto an elbow, he gazed across the spring. "I will check."

"You rest, pard," Clay reverted to English. "I'll take a look-see."

The cave narrowed at the rear, forming a dark pocket partially blocked by the spring. Keeping his feet close to the wall, Clay moved around the pool. The ceiling became so low that he had to stoop. Despite the obvious—that there was no passageway—he groped every square inch of the rough wall. At length he sighed and returned to the main chamber. "There is only the footpath," he announced in Chiricahua, then, for Marista's benefit, added, "It looks as if those soldier boys have us over a barrel. Unless we can sprout wings and fly, our goose is cooked."

152

"Goose?" she repeated.

"We don't stand a snowball's chance in hell," Clay amended while stepping close to the entrance. He refused to accept that they were beaten. If there was one lesson his pa had impressed on him again and again and again, it was that the Taggert clan weren't a bunch of quitters.

Clay had lost track of the number of times he had figured to cash in his chips, only to have his fat pulled out of the fire at the last minute. Grit and clever wits had saved him before; maybe they could do so again.

Rising on tiptoe, Clay scanned the path. Dozens of rifles glistened in the sunlight at the bottom of the spire. Venturing out there invited swift execution. Yet there was no other way down. They were trapped! How long before he was willing to admit the truth to himself? he wondered.

Exasperated, Clay rubbed his chin and idly raised his head to look up at the sky. The ceiling of the cave, which was no more than ten feet above him, limited his view. Like a bolt out of the blue, an idea struck him, and he nearly made the fatal mistake of stepping to the very edge to study the spire above.

Cuchillo Negro had been watching intently. "You have an idea, White Apache?"

"Yes," Clay said. "Has anyone ever tried to climb around to the other side of Eagle's Roost?"

"No one who wanted to live," Cuchillo Negro said with a straight face.

"I am serious," Clay insisted. "We can wait for the sun to set, then work our way around and down. The white-eyes are all on this side of the spire. We can slip right out from under their noses."

"The stone is too smooth," Ponce interjected. "Not even mountain sheep could do it."

Clay moved to the right-hand corner and craned his neck for a glimpse of the outer surface. Thin cracks laced the stone, but he couldn't tell if they were wide enough to allow a person to gain purchase or strong enough to hold the weight of a full-grown man.

The crack of a shot from down in the canyon fell on Clay's ears at the selfsame instant a bullet buzzed past his ear and bit into the cave wall. The whine of the ricochet was like a piercing whistle. A fraction of a second later, Colletto yipped in pain.

Clay crouched, realizing that he had nearly had his fool head blown off. He scooted over to the Pimas, where Marista was examining a crease on the boy's shoulder. The spent slug had torn the skin but done no real damage.

Cuchillo Negro came over, his countenance sober. "I agree with you, Lickoyee-shis-inday, that we must act before the white-eyes think to use the cave to their advantage."

Clay was about to ask what the warrior meant when the answer hit him. All the soldiers had to do was fire sustained volleys into the cave until eventually the ricochets wiped out every last one of them.

"As for climbing down the other side," Cuchillo Negro went on, "for the boy it would be impossible. I think it would sap the strength of the woman, and she would fall long before she reached the bottom. Delgadito, in his condition, would not get halfway."

The warrior had given an accurate assessment of factors that Clay in his enthusiasm had failed to take into account. But he wasn't ready to abandon the plan. "One of us has to try. Since the idea was mine, I will be the one. *Shee-dah.*"

Marista faced him, her eyes pools of worry.

Deliberately not meeting her gaze, Clay said, "If I make it down, I'll find a way to lure most of the boys in blue off. When the times comes, you will know it. Be ready."

"You risk all," Cuchillo Negro said.

"I led us here."

Aware of the woman's eyes boring into him, Clay stepped to the pool and splashed water on his face and neck. He saw no reason to mention that he had long been skittish of heights, and as a sprout he had never dared climb high into trees for fear of falling. It had taken every ounce of self-control he had to climb the path to the cave. For the life of him he didn't see how he was going to climb down the spire, but he had to do it. There was no shirking his responsibility.

Soon breakfast was ready. The food took Clay's mind off the frightful feat he had set for himself. As he downed his third cup of piping hot black coffee, he was taken aback to hear his name being shouted outside.

Setting down the battered tin cup, Clay hurried over. So did the others. Leery of a ruse to draw him into the open, he halted a few feet from where the rock path merged into the cave.

"Clay Taggart!" the hail was repeated. "This is Capt. Gerald Forester, Fifth Cavalry Flying Detachment speaking. If you're up there, give a holler."

Cupping a hand to his mouth, Clay replied, "I'm here! What do you want?"

"Step out where I can see you."

Clay laughed long and loud. "What do you take me for, Captain? A damned greenhorn?"

"I give you my personal word of honor that none of my troopers will fire," the officer bellowed. Then, lowering his voice just a little, "Did you hear that, men? Anyone who fires faces a court martial when we get back to the post."

Intrigued, Clay inched forward until he could see a lone figure standing on the footpath. The officer spotted him and held out his hands to show they were empty.

"What do you want, Captain?"

"To save us both a lot of aggravation. You can't come down, we can't come up. But we can wait you out. So why not make it easy on yourself and surrender? I promise to see you safely to Fort Bowie to stand trial. Beyond that, it's out of my hands."

"Why all this concern for my welfare?" Clay asked.

"To be honest, mister, I'd rather string you up from the handiest tree. Or let my men use you for a pincushion. You're scum, a traitor to your own kind, and you deserve to be exterminated."

Forester pushed his hat back. "But I can't let my personal feelings dictate my actions. I'm a soldier. And I don't care to have my men and animals roast under this broiling sun any longer than they have to. So what do you say? Give it up. You're butchering days are over, one way or the other. You might as well make it easy on yourself and the bucks with you."

Clay had to smile at the officer's audacity. "I'm not about to surrender, not until I've settled accounts with Miles Gillett."

"The rancher? What the hell does he have to do with any of this?"

"Everything. He framed me. Made me an outlaw."

"It won't wash, Taggart. He sure as hell didn't make you join a band of renegade Apache."

Clay knew that to try and explain would be wasted effort. "Have it your way, Captain. I'm not giving up." A thought pricked him. "But I would like to let the woman and boy come down, if you'll pledge to release them. They had no part in any of the killings."

The officer stiffened. "There's a woman and child up there? Damn. I didn't know. Who are they?"

"A Pima and her son. What do you say?"

"Unlike some I could mention, I don't make war on females or kids. Send them down."

Nodding, Clay turned. Forester struck him as being honorable enough, as a man who could be trusted, within limits. Marista and Colletto would be safe. But he saw right away by the set of her jaw that she wasn't about to go. "It's for your own good," he urged.

"No."

"Think of your son. He has his whole life ahead of him. Why have him die when there is no need?"

"Son not want go. I not leave you. He not leave me." A hint of fear crept into her tone. "You want me go? Like Culozul?"

Although he knew he should tell her that he did, Clay couldn't bring himself to mouth the words. She had been betrayed once; he'd be damned if he was going to make her suffer the same agony again. "I do not," he said softly.

Heartfelt gratitude radiated from her features. Marista placed a hand on his wrist and said tenderly, "Thank you. I tell you before. You be good man."

Troubled and pleased at the same time, Clay

swiveled and regarded the waiting officer a few moments. "I wish they would come but they won't. They aim to see this through to the end."

Forester's shoulders slumped. "I'm sorry to hear that, Taggart. I truly am. Ask them one more time. Beg them if you have to."

"It wouldn't do any good."

The officer nodded. "So be it. But you have to understand my position. We have enough water to last us three days at the most, not taking into account the time it will take us to reach the nearest stream once we leave. I don't have any choice."

"What are you getting at?"

"Just this," Captain Forester said. Whirling, he shouted for all the troopers to hear, "Open fire!"

Chapter Twelve

For all of two seconds the White Apache stood riveted in shock at the officer's abrupt turn-around. Then, as dozens of carbines cracked in booming cadence and slugs filled the cave mouth or chipped at the ceiling and floor, he threw himself to the rear. A shot stung his arm, another his calf, but neither did more than draw trickles of blood.

The Chiricahuas and the Pimas also fell back, bending low to keep from being hit by the scores of rounds that ricocheted throughout the cave. Lead flew back and forth, up and down, at all angles.

Ponce suddenly held out a bleeding hand and shook it.

Cuchillo Negro hit the floor and rolled toward the spring.

Delgadito was moving as fast as he could, a

hand wedged against the bandage to staunch the renewed flow of blood.

"All the way to the rear!" Clay directed, first in English, then in the Chiricahua tongue. The band obeyed, the warriors allowing the woman and her boy to precede them.

Miniature geysers burst from the pool as bullet after bullet pockmarked its surface. Some of the water splashed onto White Apache's feet, nearly causing him to slip on the slick floor.

Then they reached the sanctuary of the pocket and huddled together, shoulder to shoulder, White Apache and the warriors on the outside, protecting the Pimas with their own bodies.

The firing went on and on. Hundreds, perhaps thousands of rounds were expended. Bits of stone rained from the ceiling and the walls. Small clouds of dust formed, hugging the floor like fog.

White Apache grew enraged at the officer's callous disregard for the welfare of Marista and Colletto. He couldn't help questioning whether Forester would have given the order to fire if the pair had been white and not Pimas. Maybe the captain was one of those who believed all Indians should be exterminated like lice, regardless of whether they were women, men, or children.

White Apache made a vow. If he lived, he would make it a point to track down Capt. Gerald Forester and repay the man for the cold-blooded deed done this day.

After what seemed like half an hour, the firing ceased. Clay motioned for the others to stay put and dashed to the rim. The soldiers were taking a breather, perhaps to let their guns cool, since overheated carbines had a tendency to jam. Or maybe they were conserving ammunition. He saw

Forester surveying the cave through field glasses and couldn't resist popping up just to let the man know they were still alive.

"Fire at will! Now! Quickly!"

The troopers had to scramble to load and shoot, giving White Apache more time than he needed to reach the pocket. The shooting went on twice as long. Cuchillo Negro was the only one hit, suffering a flesh wound.

At last quiet reined. White Apache moved to the front of the spring and drank. Crawling to the entrance, he spied on the Flying Detachment without revealing himself.

Down below, Capt. Forester was in a quandary. He was confident that the steady firing had killed or maimed most of the renegades since it was unthinkable that any living creature could have survived, but he couldn't bring himself to send any men up the footpath, not yet, if there was a chance that even one of the renegades lived. A single warrior could pick off anyone who tried to reach the cave.

Forester had to content himself with waiting. He moved among the troopers, complimenting them on a job well done. It was important to keep their morale high, to remind them that they were dealing with the worst cutthroats in Arizona Territory. Much to his relief, no one asked him about the woman and child. It tore him up inside knowing that he had weighed their lives in the balance and decided that eliminating the renegades took priority.

Unknown to the officer, a quarter of a mile away Fiero had heard the shooting and stopped in his tracks. He had outdistanced the scouts, who were poking about in a large cluster of boulders where he had left a few clear footprints pointing in the wrong direction to tantalize them. Sooner or later they would figure out the ruse. In the meantime, he would check on the others. On all fours he slipped into dense brush, then rose and sped toward the rear of the stone spire.

Up in the cave, White Apache rested his chin on his forearms and waited for Forester's next move. Cuchillo Negro joined him without speaking. For over two hours they lay in the sun, and just when White Apache thought that the worst was over, the captain ordered his men to resume firing.

Twice more that day the same tactic was repeated. After each onslaught White Apache crept to the entrance to watch. Finally his patience was rewarded.

It was half an hour before sunset when Capt. Forester decided the time had come. There had been no sign of life in the cave. None of the volleys had been answered. Acting on the assumption the renegades were riddled with bullets, he turned to Sgt. McKinn and ordered, "Send four men up. Have the rest ready to give covering fire, just in case."

White Apache quivered when the quartet began to climb the path. He looked at Cuchillo Negro and said, "Wait until they are too high to jump."

It was like shooting clay pigeons. The four soldiers had no chance at all. Two of them dropped, shot through the head, and the other two whirled to flee. They were each drilled between the shoulder blades. Too late, the Detachment opened fire.

Capt. Forester was furious, but there was nothing he could do. He had run out of ideas and daylight, and if he wasn't careful he would run out of ammo before too long.

For White Apache, sundown was the moment

162

he had waited for. He wiped the sweat from his limbs with a piece of cloth, swallowed a cup of water, and went to the corner of the cave without speaking. No words were needed. They all knew what was at stake, what he had to do, or else.

White Apache had made a sling for his Winchester out of strips of rawhide. He slung the rifle now, eased to the edge, and reached out, seeking a handhold. There was one, a horizontal fissure with sharp edges. Taking a firm grip, he gingerly extended his foot and located a spiny knob.

Don't look down! White Apache's mind shrieked as he took a deep breath and stepped out into space, clinging to the side of the spire like an oversized lizard. He pressed his body flush and felt goosebumps cover his skin. He had to close his eyes a few moments before he could muster the courage to go on.

Locking his left hand on the fissure, White Apache extended his right as far as it would go and felt for another handhold. He found none, and feared the band was doomed. As he brought the hand toward him, he brushed a crack barely wide enough for his fingertips. It was all he had to work with so he inserted his fingers and slid farther from the opening.

And so it went. Slow inch by slow inch, every muscle as rigid as piano wire, every nerve frayed to the breaking point, never knowing if the next breath might be his last, White Apache worked his way around the spire.

The darkness helped some; it hid the bottom. White Apache could glance down without having to worry about becoming dizzy. Once on the far side there was the temptation to go faster, which he resisted. Nor would he move a hand or foot unless the other hand and foot had firm support. Several times handholds and thin ledges crumpled to dust when he applied pressure, but he was braced and didn't lose his balance.

To the east a quarter moon arced into the heavens. It had climbed to the apex of its circuit when, much to White Apache's amazement, he lowered his left leg for what must have been the two hundredth time and his sole made contact with what felt like terra firma.

Elated, White Apache shifted the moccasin to the right and the left to verify he had found footing on the ground and not merely a wide ledge. Daring to lift his cheek from the spire, he saw a few bushes nearby.

As if the drain in a wash basin had been pulled, all the strength ebbed from White Apache and he sank to the ground, exhausted, his body slick with perspiration. Lowering his forehead to the dirt, he made no attempt to go on. There was no rush. He could spare a few minutes to recover from the nightmare.

Presently White Apache girded himself and stood. The air felt deliciously cool and he took several invigorating breaths. Then, unslinging the Winchester, he turned to the south and moved around the bottom of the spire.

White Apache was a credit to the warriors who had taught him. He made as little noise as would Delgadito or Fiero or any true Chiricahua. Stopping often to look and listen to insure he wouldn't blunder onto concealed troopers, he covered scores of yards and was approaching the southwest side of Eagle's Roost when a low cough glued him in place.

Patience was an Apache virtue honed to a degree few whites could match. White Apache had learned its value and worked hard to imitate the example of his red brothers. He practiced it now, remaining in a crouch for minutes on end, heedless of a cramp in his thigh that grew worse as time went by. Only when the cough was repeated and he pinpointed the position of the soldier did he flatten and move off in another direction.

It soon became apparent he had stumbled on the last man in a long line of troopers partially ringing the spire. White Apache swung wide, moving on his toes and fingers, resembling nothing so much as a gigantic gila monster as he scuttled from cover to cover.

After a while, convinced he had gone far enough, White Apache rose to his knees and debated the best course of action to take. He had promised Marista and the rest that he would draw the troopers away from the footpath. But how should he go about it?

Then a nicker wafted on the breeze, and White Apache smiled. The cavalrymen were many miles from the nearest post. The last thing they would want would be for their mounts to run off. It would mean a long forced march with no food and little water. They would keep that from happening at all costs.

White Apache stalked toward the horses. Soon he heard the sounds typical of a large group of horses, and low voices. Lowering his belly to the ground, he wriggled toward a cluster of brush. The next moment one of the bushes uncoiled, flattened, and came toward him.

White Apache had the Winchester in front of him. All he had to do was point and fire. He started to, when a whisper no louder than the murmuring breeze revealed it wasn't an enemy.

"Lickoyee-shis-inday! I thought you were still in the cave."

"Fiero!" White Apache whispered, and clasped the warrior's wrist. "We feared you were dead."

Fiero was moved by the show of affection but he did not betray his feelings. It was unseemly for a warrior to display emotion so openly. White Apache did so often, which Fiero blamed on the man's flawed upbringing. The whites did not know how to do anything right. "Are the others with you?"

In a few words, White Apache explained.

Incredulous, Fiero craned his head and stared up at the stone spire, which seemed to touch the stars themselves. It astounded him that anyone would attempt to climb down from so lofty a height. He knew that he would never have attempted it, and his estimation of Lickoyee-shis-inday rose a notch.

"I have a plan," White Apache added. He shared his thoughts on the horses.

"We think alike," Fiero said. "That is why I am here."

"We will work together."

Side by side, the pair advanced. Once in the brush, they crept another twenty-five yards, to the lip of a shallow hollow, where they saw the string tethered under the watchful eyes of three soldiers, two of whom were talking beside some mesquite while the third made a circuit of the restless animals.

Using hand signs, White Apache conveyed his intent. Fiero slipped off without a word.

After waiting a few moments, White Apache angled toward the pair of unsuspecting troopers. He smelled the acrid odor of smoke. An orange dot flared in the night, revealing why; one of the soldiers was enjoying a cigarette.

Enough mesquite lined the hollow to permit White Apache to creep within ten feet of his quarry. Lying the Winchester at his side, he drew his Bowie knife.

The taller trooper was speaking quietly. "—told me the captain wasn't very upset about Parmalee. Which ain't surprising. The two of them never did get along very well."

"Forester was sure as hell upset at the scouts, though," said the other man. "He couldn't see how they lost the trail."

"If you ask me, the savages are all in cahoots, the renegades and the tame bucks alike," declared the tall one. "The only way to stop this bloodshed is to wipe every last Injun off the face of the earth."

White Apache noted that the short man had placed the stock of his carbine on the ground, that the tall man had his in the crook of an arm. Both wore revolvers but the flaps to their holster were closed. No matter what, he had to keep them from squeezing off a shot.

Like a mountain lion waiting for the moment when its prey would be most vulnerable, White Apache bided his time.

"I just hope we finish off the stinking renegades soon, Garth," the short man said.

"Me too, Brett. I never thought I'd say this, but I'm actually looking forward to being at Fort Bowie."

Brett pivoted and surveyed the hollow. "Say, where the hell did Winslow get to? He was over there a second ago."

Garth shifted to look, which put the backs of both men to White Apache. Instantly he rose and sprang, taking three lightning bounds. He speared the Bowie into Garth's ribs, felt the edge scrape bone, and heard the gasp Garth uttered as the point pierced his heart.

Wrenching the blade out, White Apache spun to dispatch the short one, but Brett was too quick for him and sidestepped the thrust. The trooper tried to bring his carbine to bear but his foot caught on a plant, and he fell. White Apache pounced as Brett frantically scrambled upright.

The soldier opened his mouth to shout for help. Automatically White Apache slammed a knee into Brett's groin so that the only sound that came out was a strangled whine. Flicking his arm, White Apache cut the man's shoulder, and Brett, desperately darting aside, lost his grip on the carbine.

White Apache could not give the man a moment's respite. He attacked, swinging waist height to keep Brett from unlimbering the Colt. The soldier dodged, twisted, feinted right and went left. White Apache missed him by a hair. Again Brett threw back his head to shout. This time White Apache snapped his right arm to his shoulder and let the Bowie fly.

The blade flashed like a meteor, impaling itself to the hilt in the man's jugular. Brett, shocked, halted and grabbed the hilt. Gurgling and spitting, he tore the knife free. A torrent of blood spewed in its wake.

White Apache raised a fist to batter the man senseless, but no further blows were needed. The trooper sagged, blubbering softly, his eyelids fluttering. White Apache snatched the Bowie and stood aside while the man sank onto his side and died within seconds in a spreading crimson pool.

White Apache wiped the Bowie clean on

Garth's shirt, retrieved the Winchester, and turned to the horses. From out of the darkness whisked Fiero, the new loop-style cartridge belt adorning his muscular midsection ample evidence that the other guard had been disposed of.

"Now we drive the horses off!"

"No."

"No?"

"Now we stampede them straight past Eagle's Roost," White Apache said, and Fiero grinned, understanding. Moving slowly forward so as not to spook the animals, they each picked a horse and cut it loose from the string.

White Apache freed the rest of the animals while Fiero sat ready to chase any inclined to run off. None did, although many were agitated by the scent of blood. White Apache rode to the west side of the hollow, directly across from Fiero and near the rear of the herd.

Suddenly White Apache spied a pair of figures approaching on the run from the direction of the spire. Waving his rifle to signal Fiero, he rose up off his bay, yipped shrilly, and banged three swift shots into the air. Fiero followed his lead. The result was exactly what they wanted.

The herd broke into motion. With one accord the dozens of horses fled on out of the hollow, pounding up and over the side, making for Eagle's Roost in a milling mass of drumming hoofs and flying manes and tails. Panicked whinnies rent the air.

White Apache jabbed his heels into the bay and stayed abreast of the herd. He saw the approaching figures dash eastward to get out of the way of the horses, heard rough shouts that were answered from the vicinity of the spire. Fiero's

169

rifle boomed and one of the figures dropped. The other dived behind a bush and brought a six-shooter into play.

Whooping and hollering, White Apache spurred the herd to greater speed. As he had hoped, the animals were spreading out. They were also raising tremendous amounts of dust that choked the air. In no time he could hardly see more than fifteen feet with any clarity.

Gunfire blasted, courtesy of troopers firing wildly, the shots for the most part going high.

Through a break in the dust, White Apache spotted nine or ten soldiers running to meet the herd. The men were yelling and waving and jumping up and down, trying to stop the animals. He shouted louder and emptied the Winchester to keep the horses stampeding, and they did.

The dust grew thicker. A trooper materialized directly ahead, turning every which way as if uncertain which route offered safety. He spied White Apache and clawed at the pistol on his hip.

Without slowing, White Apache galloped past, swinging the rifle like a club. The impact lifted the man off his feet and left him sprawled senseless.

A gruff voice rose above the riot of noise.

"After them! Don't let the horses get away!"

Off to the right several soldiers were sprinting in pursuit of the herd. White Apache reined up so they wouldn't spot him and sought to get his bearings. By his reckoning he was west of the spire by no more than thirty or forty yards. Drawing his Colt, White Apache trotted toward it.

The bay unaccountably shied. White Apache looked down to find the battered body of a scout lying face down. The Indian had been trampled to death. He went a little farther and saw another trooper limping to the north.

A flurry of shots reminded White Apache that not all the troopers had gone after the herd. Moments later he came on three dead cavalrymen close to the base of the footpath. Closer still was Fiero, probing the dust cloud for more enemies.

White Apache drew rein at the very end of the path, then wheeled the bay. He was not going to budge until the rest of the band showed up, even if the entire Detachment returned.

Fiero, as usual, was aglow with the lust of battle. "Ho! It is a fine night to die!" he cried.

But no cavalrymen appeared. Gradually the dust began to settle. To the north there were curses and shouts that indicated the troopers were rounding up the horses.

White Apache anxiously watched the footpath, telling himself that it shouldn't be long, that the Pimas and the Chiricahuas would show up at any second. But another minute went by, then two, and they failed to appear. He gripped the bay's mane, about to slide off and go see what was taking them.

"Here they come!" Fiero declared.

Delgadito was in the lead, moving slowly because of his wound. Marista and the boy were next. Cuchillo Negro carried her water skin, while Ponce brought a leather pouch bulging with ammunition.

White Apache vaulted from the bay and gave it a resounding smack on the rump, sending it fleeing on the heels of the herd. Taking Marista's hand, he hastened to the southeast.

From out of the tendrils of dust a grimy trooper appeared and made the mistake of using his mouth instead of his carbine. "Hey! Over here!

The damn Apaches are getting away!" Cuchillo Negro shot the man dead.

The band raced nimbly across the canyon, Delgadito keeping up despite the shape he was in. From the shelter of high boulders they looked back and saw five or six forms moving about near the footpath.

"It will take them a while to organize," White Apache remarked. He jogged onward, knowing that several miles beyond lay country so rough that horses would be a hindrance rather than a help.

A cleft in the canyon wall brought them to a tableland, which they traversed at a pace that soon had Colletto tottering with fatigue. White Apache scooped the boy into his arms and ran on.

Within three hours they entered a maze of ravines and dry washes. White Apache halted under a rock overhang and set Colletto down. "We are safe now," he announced. "By the time the whites pick up our trail, we will be far away."

Delgadito sat down, examined his side, and grimaced. "We should never have gone to Eagle's Roost. We made the *Gans* mad."

"I will never doubt your beliefs again," White Apache said, and meant it.

Ponce voiced the question most of them had in mind. "What now, lickoyee-shis-inday? What do we do next?"

The White Apache glanced at Marista and her son, then at the warriors, and said in English to himself, "I wish to hell I knew." Changing to the Chiricahua tongue, he declared, "We will work that out later. But I can make all of you one promise."

"Which is?" Cuchillo Negro asked.

"As Fiero is so fond of saying, every day will be a good day to die."

CHEYENNE

JUDD COLE

Follow the adventures of Touch the Sky as he searches for a world he can call his own!

#3: Renegade Justice. When his adopted white parents fall victim to a gang of ruthless outlaws, Touch the Sky swears to save them—even if it means losing the trust he has risked his life to win from the Cheyenne.
__3385-2 $3.50 US/$4.50 CAN

#4: Vision Quest. While seeking a mystical sign from the Great Spirit, Touch the Sky is relentlessly pursued by his enemies. But the young brave will battle any peril that stands between him and the vision of his destiny.
__3411-5 $3.50 US/$4.50 CAN

Judd Cole

Follow the adventures of Touch the Sky as he searches for a world he can call his own!

#5: Blood on the Plains. When one of Touch the Sky's white friends suddenly appears, he brings with him a murderous enemy—the rivermen who employ him are really greedy land-grabbers out to steal the Indian's hunting grounds. If the young brave cannot convince his tribe that they are in danger, the swindlers will soak the ground with innocent blood.

__3441-7 $3.50 US/$4.50 CAN

#6: Comanche Raid. When a band of Comanche attack Touch the Sky's tribe, the silence of the prairie is shattered by the cries of the dead and dying. If Touch the Sky and the Cheyenne braves can't fend off the vicious war party, they will be slaughtered like the mighty beasts of the plains.

__3478-6 $3.50 US/$4.50 CAN

#7: Comancheros. When a notorious slave trader captures their women and children, Touch the Sky and his brother warriors race to save them so their glorious past won't fade into a bleak and hopeless future.

__3496-4 $3.50 US/$4.50 CAN

LEISURE BOOKS
ATTN: Order Department
276 5th Avenue, New York, NY 10001

Please add $1.50 for shipping and handling for the first book and $.35 for each book thereafter. PA., N.Y.S. and N.Y.C. residents, please add appropriate sales tax. No cash, stamps, or C.O.D.s. All orders shipped within 6 weeks via postal service book rate. Canadian orders require $2.00 extra postage and must be paid in U.S. dollars through a U.S. banking facility.

Name _____

Address _____

City _____ State _____ Zip _____

I have enclosed $_____in payment for the checked book(s).

Payment <u>must</u> accompany all orders.☐ Please send a free catalog.